BORDER RIDING

BORDER RIDING

by NIGEL TRANTER

Illustrated by RICHARD KENNEDY

WHITE LION PUBLISHERS LIMITED
London, Sydney and Toronto

By the same author
SPANIARDS' ISLE

First published in Great Britain
by Brockhampton Press Ltd. 1959

Text Copyright © Nigel Tranter 1959

Illustrations Copyright © Brockhampton Press Ltd. 1959

White Lion Edition 1977

ISBN 0 85686 242 8

Made and printed in Great Britain
for White Lion Publishers Limited,
138 Park Lane, London W1Y 3DD
by Hendington Limited,
Lion House, North Town, Aldershot, Hampshire

Contents

CHAPTER ONE

To Horse!

KEN RUTHERFORD met the afternoon train at the tiny station of Hangingshaws, deep amongst the green, rounded Border hills. He had had quite a job to persuade his parents to let him go and meet Fiona in the pony and trap. That was the right way for a girl like Fiona MacBride, from a far-away Hebridean island, to start her first visit to the Border-land – not to be whisked away inside a stuffy car.

Fiona was the only passenger to get down, and looked rather small and forlorn standing there alone on the platform with her bag, as the train chuffered and clanked its way southwards. But that was non-sense, for there was nothing in the least bit forlorn about Fiona, as her vivid red hair, sparkling eyes, and quick, eager ways all made clear. At sight of Ken she came running, remembered her bag, ran back for it, and then came scampering towards him, laughing at her forgetfulness.

For one horrible moment Ken was afraid that she was going so far to forget herself as to hug him – or even kiss him, which would have been far worse – but at the last yard or two she pulled up, and stood grinning. She certainly did not look in the least tired after her long journey from one end of Scotland to the other.

'Hullo, Ken!' she said. 'You don't look one bit different.'

'You look just the same, yourself,' he said. He half thought of shaking hands, but scratched his head instead.

'Do I?' Almost she seemed just a little disappointed at that. 'It's a whole year since we saw each other last at Eorsa. People can change a lot in a year, you know.'

She hoped he would say she had grown, but Ken was remembering his duty.

'Welcome to Brave Borderland, Fiona, anyway,' he said.

'Thank you. But what's brave about it, Ken?'

'Oh, well – it's just . . . brave, you know, I mean – well, you'll find out. Come on.'

'Mustn't forget my bag . . .'

'Oh, yes. Hand it over. That's our trap, out there. The pony's name is Walter Scott, by the way.'

'Goodness! Why, on earth?'

'Because, Daddy says, he takes a deal of starting – but once he does there's no beating him!'

'I think Walter Scott is lovely,' Fiona said, presently, as Ken came out with her bag. She was fondling the velvety nose of a pure white, medium-height pony, cleanly built, with wise blue eyes. 'He's so neatly made. I'm used to Highland garrons, of course – and though they are dears, they're just a little bit clumsy. I do love horses.'

'That's just as well, all things considered!' the boy said, grinning.

'Oh? I suppose so. I mean – well, is it?'

'Yes,' he said briefly. 'Jump in. D'you want to take the reins, Fiona?'

'Oh, no. I wouldn't know where to go.'

'No – but Walter Scott would! Never mind – here goes.'

There did not seem to be any station-master, or even a porter, at Hangingshaws. There was no village, either – just a single house beside the station-yard, and then the road stretching away right and left between the grassy, tree-dotted, park-like fields, all slopes and mounds and hollows, scattered with white Cheviot sheep, and all around the high green hills of the Scottish Border. The air was loud with the baaing of sheep, from near and far.

'It is lovely!' Fiona said, waving her hand at it all. 'So . . . so peaceful. And green.'

'Peaceful!' Ken snorted. 'Just you wait!' He slapped the reins on the white pony's broad rump. 'Git on, hoss – git on!'

Walter Scott certainly did not break into any gallop, there and then, but went pacing sedately out of the yard and down the road, between the bright-green June hedges, clip-clop, clip-clop. The harness creaked, and the little trap smelled of varnish and leather and new-mown hay.

'He'll pick up a bit, in a few minutes,' Ken assured, flapping the reins again. 'Once he really gets his head towards home. Look – right down there, across the river, in the trees. A good two miles away. That's Houndlaw – our farm.'

'It looks marvellous! Everything looks marvellous – lovely!' Fiona cried. 'Don't make Walter Scott hurry, Ken. I'm enjoying looking at it all, so much, I didn't realize that you had such high hills, here.'

'That's the main Cheviot range, right ahead,' he told her. 'Beyond that is England. The Border runs right along the ridge, there.'

The road was leading down a long, slow hillside into a fairly wide valley where a silver river coiled, gleaming in the afternoon sun, and beyond, out of the wooded foothills, the great thrusting shoulders of the Cheviots rose, ridge upon ridge southwards, as far as eye could see.

'England! I've never been to England,' Fiona said. 'To think it's just over there! What is it like?'

'Oh, well – it's all right, I suppose,' he told her.
'Some people quite like it. I'll take you there.'

'Oh – will you? That would be wonderful!'

'Right. We'll go. Maybe to-morrow. Get you into
training.'

'Training? Do I need training, Ken?'

'Of course you do. But you'll be all right.'

Walter Scott perked up a little, as they bowled
downhill. Ken handed the girl the reins, but she did
not have to do anything very much with them, for
Walter Scott was well able to look after himself.

'How I've been looking forward to this holiday!'
Fiona cried. 'Ever since you left Eorsa. Am I in time
to see the famous Common Riding?'

'See? You don't *see* Common Ridings – you take
part in them,' the boy answered somewhat scorn-
fully. 'You *ride* the Ridings. Of course you're in time.
It's in three days, the main affair. That's the whole
point of your coming in June. But you'll not talk
about it being so peaceful, then!'

Fiona swallowed. 'No? *Ride* it! But, Ken . . . I
don't know whether I'm able to. I mean – I'm not a
terribly good rider, really. I've ridden garrons all
my life, of course – but they are quiet, stocky beasts,
that never go above a slow trot. I wouldn't like . . .'

'Of course you're able!' the other declared.

13

'Nothing in it. So long as you can sit a horse. After that you just follow with the crowd.'

'But, even then . . .'

'Look,' the boy said strongly, 'don't be a stodge, Fiona! When I came to Eorsa I took part in all your island things, didn't I? I went out in the boat with you, in rough weather. I climbed cliffs. Well – this is what we do in the Borders.'

After that, there was nothing for the girl to say.

Down at the foot of the hill, they crossed the river by an old hump-backed bridge, and then trotted through well-tilled fields towards the farm-buildings.

At sight of the place, Fiona exclaimed. 'Goodness, I thought you lived on a farm. Not in a castle!'

'It's not a castle. All these old Border farm places started out by having keeps – fortified towers, you know – for defence during the Border wars. They just grew out of that, sticking bits on here and there, as needed. Rutherfords have been sticking bits on to Houndlaw Tower for centuries. But it's still a farm.'

'But it's thrilling! Do you mean to say that **you** really had raiders and rievers and things here, Ken?'

'Well, I'll show you where Douglas of Cavers – he was Sheriff of Teviotdale – hanged Black Wat Rutherford from his own tower for stealing somebody or other's cattle. We don't behave like that nowadays. At least, not the Rutherfords!'

Houndlaw certainly looked an exciting sort of place, with its high, old, square greystone tower and whitewashed more modern buildings – with old lawns, a duck-pond, orchards, tall sycamore trees, barns and stables, all mixter-maxter.

As they drove up, a lady appeared at the front porch. Ken waved. He had taken over the reins from Fiona, and now drove towards the back quarters.

'We'll go and see the horses, right away,' he announced. 'I want to show you Demon. He's new. Coal-black. Daddy gave him to me for my birthday.'

'Yes – but isn't that your mother, waiting for us?'

'Oh, she'll keep. You'll like Demon . . .'

'No – I think I ought to go and say how d'you do to your mother first, Ken. I really do.' Fiona insisted. 'It's only polite. Demon will keep too, won't he?'

'Oh, well . . .'

Undoubtedly it seemed that Ken Rutherford was interested in horses. It looked as though Fiona was going to be a good deal more knowledgeable about those horses, too, before this visit was over, whether she wanted to be or not.

CHAPTER TWO

Into the Hills

THAT first impression turned out to be no exaggeration. Though Ken's parents stopped him from actually getting his guest on to a horse and dashing about the countryside there and then, most of that first evening was spent in and around the stables and paddock. Mrs Rutherford explained to Fiona that he was not always so bad as this; at Common Riding time, the Borders just went mad about horses – and there was nothing to be done about it. She had come from Edinburgh herself, to Houndlaw, and had had to learn the same lesson.

In the morning, Ken came to Fiona's room with an old pair of his sister's riding breeches for her, and had her into the saddle before breakfast. There was a good deal of argument, even so, about a mount for her. Fiona blankly refused the honour of trying out Ken's Demon, who looked far too spirited and dashing for her to do more than cautiously pat. And even the smaller and quieter chestnut mare that had been Ken's favourite companion until this black thing came along seemed a bit much to her. She did what she could by agreeing to ride Walter Scott, who was trained for the saddle as well as the shafts – and in fact had been the boy's first mount. He would make a suitably safe and sober steed, surely – however scornful his former master was of her riding him.

Practically all day, then, Fiona was ridden here and there, made to jump this ditch – hanging on for dear life – splash across that river, clamber through gaps in walls, open gates from the saddle, and so on. She made no complaints – in fact she enjoyed every minute of it. Or nearly. But by evening she was distinctly sore and stiff – and walked as though she was. Ken's only comment to this was that it proved how right he had been that she needed to get into training. She would thank him on Common Riding day.

Fiona kept her own opinion about that. She was beginning to wonder whether this Common Riding business was going to be more trouble than it was worth.

It rained hard that night, and wakening, listening to the downpour, Fiona got the notion that perhaps this might spare her another day in the saddle. Her aching body would be glad enough of that – but she wasn't quite so sure what her *mind* wanted.

But, in the morning, there were no doubts. It was

a bright, cool, breezy day – just the weather for the hills, Ken announced. They would take a picnic, and ride quietly over the route to be taken by the Rule-kirk Cornet and his mounted followers next day, so that Fiona would know it and be prepared.

The girl moistened her lips, and wondered whether, if they were going to be riding all day to-morrow too, it might not be a good idea just to have a rest to-day?

Ken stared at her, shocked.

'Rest!' he repeated. 'You didn't come all the way here from the Hebrides to *rest*, did you? I thought you would *like* to get some guidance about to-morrow's ride? And didn't you want to cross the Border into England?'

'Will we be doing that to-day?' she asked.

'That's the idea, anyway,' she was told. 'We'll ride right up to the main Cheviot ridge there, on the side of Peel Fell. You can just see it from here – on the skyline. It's about ten miles. Up Rule Water, and back down Jed Water. You'll love it.'

Ken's parents seemed to be quite used to this sort of thing, and not in the least worried about dangers or distances. Their only concern was that he did not overtire Fiona, and took no risks in the high peat-bogs up on the summit plateau.

18

So, well stocked up with food and matches and thermos-flasks in their saddle-bags, they set off southwards. Ken had wanted Fiona to ride the chestnut mare to-day, claiming that Walter Scott would be much too slow; but the girl had stuck to the white pony determinedly. She and Walter Scott were becoming firm friends.

They rode through a sparkling morning, up amongst grassy foothills where golden gorse-bushes crackled in the warm sunshine, beside tinkling, twinkling streams and past neat plantations and shelter-belts of mixed trees, where the cuckoos called hauntingly and were echoed by the sheep that baaed on every hillside.

As they went, Ken told Fiona something about the Common Ridings. Enthusiastic as he was, he could not tell her it all, of course, for it was a very big subject, with its roots deep in past history. But he explained enough to give her some idea of what would happen to-morrow, and why: how all the Scots Border burghs, like Rulekirk, held these hard-riding festivals in the early summer – and how, curiously, none of the English boroughs on the other side of the Cheviots did. How they all owned wide common lands, in the old days, and it was necessary for the townspeople to ride round these each year, marking the boundaries, to thwart the attempts of neighbouring lairds and landowners who were always trying to steal the common lands.

'But surely they don't have to do that nowadays?' Fiona protested. 'People don't steal land nowadays.'

'Well, no,' Ken admitted. 'But it's a good custom to keep up. It keeps everybody interested in their burgh's common lands and history, you see. And it's a wonderful excuse for fun and games and high jinks – feasts, horse-racing, and excitement. There's a good lot of speech-making, too,' he added, less keenly. 'You see, it helps to keep traditions alive – which most people think is a good thing. Each burgh's festival is linked to some happening in the town's history – usually to do with the old Border wars and forays. Ours, at Rulekirk, commemorates the Rescue of Rulehead Rab. Rab Turnbull of Rule-head – that's just up here, in front of us – was captured, with a lot of his cattle, by a band of raiding English, and was being carried away over the Border. A group of young men – callants we call them – rode out from Rulekirk town after them, and gave the raiders a real bashing, just up there on the side of Peel Fell, where we're going. They took prisoner Sir Thomas Heron, the English leader, and eventually ransomed him for stacks of gold. That was about 1570. With the money, they started a fund for educating the poor boys of Rulekirk – and now the town has got the best and richest school in the Borders,' Ken added with pride.

'Well – a rum way of starting a school, I must say,' said Fiona. 'I bet they teach a lot of history there! And they ride up here every year, in memory of it?'

'That's right. There's a ceremony, where the battle took place. You'll enjoy it – lots of fun. Mock fights. Races. Sing-songs. Everybody picnics. But it's a fairly rough ride up, as you'll see. I mean, when the pace is hot.'

Fiona did see it – all too clearly. It was as well

that Walter Scott was not only surefooted but refused to be hurried. They did not follow any road or track here, but just rode over the grassy, tussocky uplands, climbing and climbing. Mile after mile they went, and the outspread, rolling Borderland sank away below them, all valleys and ranges and rivers and fields, with little Rulekirk smoking away over on their right. Ken fretted a bit, at the pace, holding his spirited black in – though he occasionally gave the handsome creature its head for a brisk canter, or even a short gallop. He then had to come riding back for Fiona, who, like her careful mount, was not

impressed by such displays of speed. A nice, steady trot was as much as either of them would rise to.

They reached the head-waters of Jed about noon, climbing steeply now, along what Ken said was an old Roman road, mossy and broken. An hour later they rode up on to the main summit ridge of the Cheviot range, high up on the shoulder of massive Peel Fell, fully seventeen hundred feet above the sea. Far and wide the land stretched beneath them, on every hand, to the blue of the sea itself, away to the east at Berwick-on-Tweed.

Ken pulled up, and dismounted.

'Well, how d'you like it?' he demanded.

'Oh, it's wonderful, Ken – just wonderful!' said Fiona. 'What a view! And what a lot of sky! And land. Look at all those little towns, back there. I can count four – no, five . . .'

'Och, yes. But that's not what I mean. Look this other way. In front. Does it not feel any different?'

'Different? How d'you mean?'

'Well, you're in England, now.'

'Goodness me – is that right? But how? Where? I didn't see anything . . .'

'See that big stone, back there? And that cairn, down the hill? Well, the Border-line runs between them. We crossed it about a hundred yards back.'

'Mercy on us – and I didn't know! Is that all? It feels just the same . . .' Fiona stared in front of her. 'All that spread of hills – that is England? I thought England was a flat place, all cities and factories and village greens and things?'

23

'Not Northumberland, anyway,' the boy assured her. 'Nor Cumberland, either. They're almost as good as Scotland, really. Let's have lunch. This is the site of the battle – or the Rescue, anyway.'

'Let's. I could eat a horse!' Fiona agreed.

'You'd have a long walk home, in that case! And I guess Walter Scott would be sort of tough! Better with a sandwich. Come on.'

They made a fire of dead heather stems – for it was cold up there in the searching wind of the high places. The plan was to wait there for about an hour, to give the horses a good rest – for they had come fully ten miles – and then to ride up to the top of Peel Fell. These Cheviot Hills were round and fairly smooth, and good for riding on, so long as the peat-bogs were avoided.

But before the hour was up, Ken was stamping out the embers of the fire, and saying that they should move. The sun had gone. It was colder – but that was not what worried him most: it was the grey lowering look of the sky, to the west. It might come to nothing – but better to be on their way.

Ken did not lead back the way that they had come, but north by east, round the northern flank of Peel Fell, between it and another thrusting hill called Hartshorn Pike, less high but more pointed.

This col, or pass, would bring them through to the head of the Black Burn, which in turn would lead them down nicely to the main Jedburgh–Carter Bar road – the quickest way off the open hill. Ken, though adventurous, was not foolhardy where weather on the high tops was concerned. His father had taught him well.

Before they reached the col, looking back they saw that the distant peaks of Greatmoor, Cauld-cleuch, and Tudhope, away to the west, were all swallowed up. They had been clear before.

'Is it going to rain, Ken?' Fiona asked.

'I hope so!' the boy said – to her surprise. 'A little rain won't do us any harm.'

But it did not rain. What Ken had been afraid of, but had not mentioned, happened instead. The mist closed down on them, just after they were through the pass. It came suddenly, like a grey-white curtain of cotton-wool.

'Ken,' Fiona said, after a silent moment or two. 'This isn't good – is it? Mist. Up here.'

'Och, it's just the tail-end of a cloud,' he assured, as lightly as he could. 'Though, mind you, I'd rather have had a nice brisk shower of rain. You keep close to my tail, will you?'

He urged Demon onward, but at a slow walk now.

CHAPTER THREE

Lost in the Mist

THE mist swirled and streamed around them
eerily, so thick that they could not see more than a
few feet, blanketing everything, not only from sight
but from hearing, so that the only sounds that
reached their ears were the hollow clop-clop of their
mounts' hooves on turf, and the creak of saddlery.
All else – the sigh of the wind, the wheepling of the
curlews, the trilling of larks, and the chuckling of
the many burns – was dead, gone.

Slowly they paced on, with Ken turning his head
this way and that, sniffing the air, listening, trying
to gain some idea of direction.

'How can you see where you're going?' the girl
demanded.

'I can't,' Ken admitted. 'I'm trying to use the
wind, and the slope of the ground, and the *feel* of
things . . .'

The trouble was, the wind seemed to have dropped
away entirely. Though the mist streamed past as
though driven by something, it eddied and swirled in

no one direction. No amount of holding up damped fingers to tell by the cold feeling which way the wind blew was any help. Nor was there any hint of where the sun might be.

Soon Ken dismounted to lead Demon, explaining that he could better test and recognize the rise and fall of the ground level on foot. He began to whistle a tune – but it made only a thin and lonely sound, and soon he gave it up.

There was no sort of path to follow, and Fiona had no idea what their route should be. But she was rather surprised when, after a bit, it became clear that they were gradually beginning to climb again. She had quite a job with herself not to suggest to Ken that surely this shouldn't be.

Before long, the boy halted of his own accord.

'You know,' he said, 'I think we ought to wait for a bit. Take a rest, and see if it lifts. We've plenty of time, and it probably won't stay thick like this for very long.'

'I think so, too,' Fiona agreed.

'We're definitely climbing – and we shouldn't be,' he explained. 'We should be heading down now, towards the head of the Black Burn. The trouble is, I don't know *what* we're climbing! We must have swung either to the right or the left. So it might be

the main ridge between Peel Fell and Carter Fell –
or it might be Hartshorn Pike. Or even Carlin's
Tooth, which is farther on a bit. It's maddening not
to know whether we're facing north or south!'

'I'm all for waiting,' the girl told him. 'There's
no point in getting deeper and deeper into these
hills. It's not like being out in a boat – when we'd at
least have a compass.'

'Yes – I suppose I really should carry a compass
with me,' Ken admitted. 'But I've never known it
quite so thick as this . . .'

Fiona got down, and they sat on the tussocky
grass, which the two horses nibbled away at un-
concernedly. For a while they stared blankly at the
mist that poured and rolled so busily, so silently,
around them. It was three o'clock.

28

Ken, to pass the time and keep their minds occupied, began to tell Fiona stories and legends of the old-time Borderland. He seemed to know a vast number of these. Every hillside and valley and stream and bog appeared to have a tale attached to it – of battle and bloodshed, heroism and treachery, raiding and rieving and sudden death – even the very place they were in. He certainly kept the girl from thinking too much about their present position, but on the other hand, he soon had her seeing all sorts of alarming characters and shapes and forms in the curious swirls of the mist. It was chilly enough, sitting there in that clammy air, high up as they were, without his making her blood run cold with the gruesome activities of all these old Borderers.

After a while, neither of them could pretend not to

be worried about the passage of time. They had waited for nearly two hours – and still there was no sign of the mist thinning. They could not remain here much longer.

'I think we should take a chance on making a move,' Ken said at length. 'I only wish I knew whether one was likely to swing left or right. They say that everybody, when they can't see, turns one way or the other. If we went right then obviously we're up on Peel Fell again, facing south, in which case we'd better turn back and try to keep going downhill. On the other hand, if we swung left we're up on the side of either Hartshorn or Carlin's Tooth, facing north. We *want* to go north – but not by climbing up and over a hill-top. I think, either way, we should turn and try to keep going downhill – try to get into the foot of the pass that we must have strayed out of. Once there, we'll have to decide whether to turn left or right – whichever seems to lead most down the way.'

That sounded sensible. They moved on again, a little stiffly now, leading their horses. Walter Scott kept nuzzling his soft nose into Fiona's shoulder, as though glad of her company in these strange conditions.

But, however sensible, Ken's plan did not work

out. They kept trying to go downhill – but however they turned, they seemed, sooner or later, to be faced with climbing again. They felt as though they had got trapped in the foot of a great basin, and the only way out was up the sides of it. No downhill slope lasted for any distance.

'If only we could find a burn,' Ken said. 'Water always flows downhill. If we could stick to its side, however it wandered, it would be bound to bring us to low ground.'

But, though those hills seemed to have been criss-crossed with scores of streams before, not a sign of running water could they find now anywhere.

'This is no good,' the boy decided at last. 'We're not getting anywhere. I just haven't a clue which way to turn.'

'So we're lost!' Fiona said, matter-of-factly.

'No, of course we're not lost!' he objected. 'We know where we are, pretty well. I mean, to a mile or two. All we don't know is which way to move, to get out of it!'

'Ah – that makes all the difference!' the girl said. She even managed a little smile. 'I think we should just stay where we are, Ken – just the same. So that we keep *on* knowing where we are, at least!'

'No,' Ken shook his head. 'We've tried that, and

it's no good. The mist has been down now for more than three hours. It may last for a long time yet. It's all this twisting and turning that's so hopeless. I think we ought to choose one direction, and try to stick to it. Even if it does keep on leading us uphill. After all, if we keep on, pretty straight, we've got three chances out of four of getting somewhere in a few miles. North – down to the Black Burn and eventually to the Jed Water. East – to the Carter Bar road. West – a bit farther, but not much, to the Bonchester–Liddesdale road. It's only southwards that leads to nowhere, into the deep hills. I think we should take a chance. Better than sitting down doing nothing, and getting cold.'

'All right, you're the boss, Ken. Lead on, Macduff!'

Though of course he did not say so, Ken reckoned that he was lucky in his companion. Not all girls would have taken this business in the way Fiona MacBride did.

Ken knew that moss tended to grow on the unexposed faces of rocks – away from the wind. And since the prevailing winds in these parts came from the south-west, he thought that they might get some slight help from that. Unfortunately, however, none of the rocks that they came across seemed to be of the moss-bearing sort. After a bit of discussion about what seemed to be the exposed side of one or two, they chose what they hoped was a northerly course, and decided to stick to it – if they could.

Very quickly they began to climb. And they went on climbing, too.

It was a long time later before Ken would admit defeat – or not exactly defeat, but an acknowledgement that either their straight line had been far from straight, or else they must indeed be heading southwards. They had climbed and climbed, sometimes in the saddle, sometimes on foot, seemingly endlessly, until, when they were almost at the point of turning back, at last the ground began to level off in front of them. Ken had feared that this might be the main Cheviot ridge surmounted again, though he had not said so; but when the land at length started to sink away ahead, it had seemed foolish not to go with it. And when, after a while, they had found a burn to lead them downwards, they had followed it gladly. But it had brought them only into a great area of black peat-bog, in which they floundered and splattered. Hurriedly they retraced their steps to firmer ground, and then tried to find a way round the obstacle. But it obviously extended right and left for a long way. Ken knew no such bog on the northern face of these hills. It seemed clear that they had crossed the main ridge, and the Border, and come down into the great summit plateau that stretched for miles and miles southwards – high, empty moorland, thick with bogs.

'I'm afraid, Fiona, that I've failed you badly,' the boy confessed, at last. 'We're back on the English side, again. That's clear now.'

'I'm glad something's clear, anyway!' the girl said, trying to sound lighthearted. 'I feel as though nothing will ever look clear to me again! What do we do now, then?'

'Well – nothing, really. I mean, in among these quaking bogs, we'd be asking for real trouble if we tried to keep going on. Only thing to do is to find a sheltered spot, and lie up till we can see again.'

'That . . . that may mean . . . to-morrow!' the girl said, swallowing something in her throat.

'Yes. I'm afraid it may. I'm sorry, Fiona – terribly sorry.'

'It's not your fault,' she told him bravely. 'You couldn't help the mist coming down like that. You've done everything you could. It's just . . . well, one of those things. What on earth will your mother and father think? They'll be awfully worried.'

34

'Not awfully, no. I don't think so,' Ken said. 'They'll be upset, of course. But they will have seen the hills get covered over, from Houndlaw. They'll know what has happened. They know that I can look after myself. It's you being uncomfortable that will make them anxious.'

'Oh, *I'll* be all right. I've spent nights out on the hill, too, at Eorsa. Fishing. Out in the boat, too. You don't think they'll start looking for us? Send out search-parties or anything?'

'Heavens, no! That would be no good at all. Nobody could find anybody else in this. They'll know that. They'd just get lost themselves. They know we've got food, and matches for a fire. We'll be fine.'

'Good! Then let's start being fine right away, shall we?' Fiona cried. 'We'll look on this as an adventure – and make the most of it.'

'Atta-girl!' Ken cheered. 'Well – first thing is to look for some nice sheltered spot to spend the night. You can be quite snug in the heather.'

It was half-past seven.

CHAPTER FOUR

The Sheep-Stealers

IT was not difficult to find a hollow amongst rocks.
They unsaddled the horses, and left them to fend for
themselves, knowing that they would not stray far
away. They set to pulling armfuls of heather, and any
dead stems that they came across they laid aside for
burning. Though it was a bit hard on the hands,
soon they had a great pile, into which they would be
able to snuggle down. The gathering of sufficient
fuel took longer, for they were going to need a lot of
dead heather-stems to keep a fire going for any length
of time. Ken decided that a good fire was necessary –

for though they had nothing to cook, it would keep them warm and cheerful. It was surprising how dry the heather remained, even in all that damp mist. The constant searching for dead stuff kept them occupied. There was no other type of fuel to be had up here.

They ate most of what remained of their picnic sandwiches and biscuits, keeping a little for the morning, and washed it down with a drink of ice-cold water from a nearby burn. Afterwards they sat, and fed, and watched the fire. They found that they were quite enjoying the experience. There was no use in fretting or worrying or wondering any more. They had done all that they could, and nothing else was required of them in the meantime. It was pleasant to sit there, soaking in the heat, up on the top of this strange, silent world of the mountains, with the horses every now and again coming up to nuzzle their backs. The beasts obviously were not going to go far from human company.

It got dark early, with all the weight of cloud around them, and the heat from the fire made them drowsy. They were tired, too. By soon after nine they bedded down. They had only their rolled-up water-proofs to use as covers, but they buried themselves deep in the pulled heather, piling it up all round and

37

about them as well as underneath. It kept the heat in remarkably well, and was as springy and comfortable as any mattress.

Just before she dozed off, Fiona spoke. 'It's a shame about the Common Riding, Ken. You'll miss it now, after all.'

'Ummm. I suppose so. You never know, though – they come up here to-morrow. We might just see something of it, as we go down. They come in the morning. Anyway, this is just about as good, isn't it? I mean, a real-life adventure. Don't you think so?'

But there was no reply from Fiona. She was fast asleep.

Ken lay awake for some time, listening to the occasional puff and sizzle of the dying fire, and the companionable sounds of the horses stirring nearby. He wondered about his parents, and what they were thinking. And then he wondered no more at all.

Two or three times during the night the boy awoke, the last time feeling distinctly stiff and chilly. He noticed, in a dreamy sort of way, that there were stars shining above him.

Next time that he wakened he knew that something had actually roused him. He sat up, the heather falling from him, and shivered. It was cold. Then he realized what had aroused him. It was the sound of sheep baaing.

He sat, blinking and yawning, trying to gather his sleepy wits. Why should baaing sheep wake him? It was the commonest sound of all the Borderland. But not at night. Sheep didn't baa in the middle of the night. And this was not just a few sheep, by the sound – it was lots of them. A large flock. That was the point that some alert part of his mind had been trying to tell the other sleepy part. It was not the usual quiet baaing of single sheep scattered over a wide area of hill, but the united protest of a large flock, all together. How could that be – in the middle of the night? Up here on the roof of the Cheviots?

It was not actually the middle of the night any more, of course. There was a sort of pale half-light – for the June night is never very dark in Scotland. Ken peered at his watch. It seemed to be just four o'clock. It would soon be sunrise. The mist had gone, and the stars overhead were paling. There was no wind, no sound on the still air but this distant noise of sheep. He could see the two horses, close at hand. Walter Scott was lying down.

After a minute or two, Ken leaned over and shook Fiona's shoulder. She wakened readily, much less owlish than he himself had been.

39

'There's something queer going on,' he told her. 'Hear all those sheep? That's a flock. Not just scattered sheep grazing on the hill. It's on the move, too, I would say. Sheep don't move by themselves at night, and set up all that row.'

'No?' Fiona picked heather seeds out of her hair. 'But . . . is it important, Ken?'

'Well – it may be. It probably means that there's somebody about, not so very far away. But it's a funny time of night to be moving sheep. It's just four o'clock.'

'It couldn't be something else? A fox, after them? Or a dog, running wild? I've heard of such things.'

'That's possible, I suppose. But I shouldn't think it's very likely.'

'Would it be so strange for somebody to want to move their sheep early? I mean, they might want to get them down to market somewhere, early in the day? Or something like that.'

'They would have rounded them up yesterday then. You can't round up sheep properly in the dark. I know. We're sheep-farmers. Even with the best dogs you'd always miss a lot. No self-respecting shepherd's going to do a thing like that. There has been a lot of sheep-stealing going on in the Cheviots, recently. I wonder . . . ?'

'Oh, I say! Do you really think . . . ?' Wide awake now, Fiona was eager to know more.

'I don't know. It might be. Worth having a look, anyhow. And even if it's all perfectly okay and on the level, it would be as well to find people – if there are any. Wouldn't it? I mean, we'd probably find the easiest and quickest way off the hill and on to a road. The mist has gone.'

'Yes. Yes, that's right. That's sensible,' agreed Fiona.

So they got up, finding themselves to be stiff and chilled, and saddled up the horses. As stars were now visible, Ken, by finding the Pole Star, up from the handle of the Plough, was able to show that the sound of the sheep came from south-westwards. On the still air sounds would carry a long way; he reckoned they might be a mile away, or more. They set out in that direction. They did not mount their horses but led them on foot, glad of the exercise to warm them up.

They had to climb a bit at first over rolling heather. As the light increased, Ken decided that he knew where he was. They were climbing an outlying shoulder of the *south* side of Peel Fell – that giant amongst the hills being unmistakable. This shoulder linked up with a lesser hill to the south, called Mid

Fell. At the far side of it rose the head-streams of the Deadwater Burn, which ran down to the Tyne, at the main Liddesdale-Tynedale road, near Deadwater Station. They must have crossed the main Cheviot ridge last evening, somewhere near the Kielder Stone, a noted landmark.

Over the top of the shoulder the sound of the sheep came to them much more clearly. Obviously they were down in the valley of the Deadwater Burn below them somewhere – but it was still too deep in shadow for them to make out anything.

They mounted, and rode downwards. Soon they came to the first ditch-like channels of the Deadwater. Fiona said that she did not like its name, or anything about it.

It was farther to those sheep than they had thought. They had to go more than another mile before they saw them. The valley of the burn had become quite deep now, and rounding a bend in it they saw where it widened out away in front of them, the white mass of a large bleating flock. Behind it were half a dozen men and some darting, barking dogs.

Ken pulled Demon to a halt.

'I don't like the look of that,' he said.

'Why not, Ken? I mean – how can you tell, from here?' asked Fiona.

'All those men,' he explained. 'Real sheep-men don't go out in squads like that. One shepherd, or at the most two, can cope with much larger flocks than that. What do they want five or six men for? And at this hour?'

'Don't ask me . . .'

'Those dogs are barking, too. Hear them? Real shepherds' dogs work silently. They may be sheep-dogs, but they're not being properly worked.'

'You think they're thieves, Ken – really? Stealing somebody else's sheep?' The girl's voice rose with excitement.

'I think there's a pretty good chance that they are.'

'Goodness! Then what can we do?'

'I don't know. But I think we've got to try and do something. The first thing, anyway, is not to let them see *us*. Not until we're sure of them.'

'Yes. Where will they be going with them? Taking the sheep?'

'If they're genuine local folk, they'll just be taking them down to some farm, or some fold or fank, for dipping. But if not, it's my guess that there will be some big motor-lorries – cattle-floats, you know – down at the road, to take them away. They'll slaughter the beasts somewhere, and sell the carcases to shady butchers and hotel-keepers. In places like Newcastle or Glasgow. That's what they do, Daddy says.'

'Can we go to the farmer, then – the owner? And warn him. Where is the farm?'

'I don't really know. It could be miles and miles away. These big Cheviot sheep-runs stretch for thousands and thousands of acres. The nearest farm, I think, is Myredykes, a couple of miles along the road from Deadwater Station – but that's on the Scots side. These won't be his sheep – we're in England still, here.'

'Is there nothing that we can do then? We can't just let them get away with all those poor sheep.' It was fairly certain that Fiona was more concerned about all the sheep getting killed than anything else.

'I'm just wondering. . . . Only thing I can think of is to go down to the road and try to stop a car. Try to get help that way. The trouble is, there's not likely to *be* any at this hour. It's never a busy road at any time.'

'But we couldn't do that, anyway,' Fiona objected. 'Not unless we're dead sure that these *are* thieves. If they are, we can hardly expect some passing motorist to get out and tackle six men single-handed. They'll be pretty tough, I expect.'

'I suppose that's true. We might get a motorist to go for the police, though.'

'Better if we could find a telephone, ourselves, down there.'

'Yes. Well – we'd better get down to the road first, whatever we do. We don't want these folk to see us, though, so we'd better go back a bit, and climb up the side of this valley on to higher ground – keeping well back, up there, so that we're out of their sight. We can work down that way. Coming?'

'Yes. How far are we from the road?' queried Fiona.

'About two or three miles, I'd say. We'll have to hurry – though we'll move an awful lot faster than these men, with their slow sheep to drive.'

So they rode up the hillside to the left, till the slope of it hid them from sight of the foot of the glen, and then headed westwards again, making for the deep wide trough of the main Tyne valley, parallel with the Deadwater, but fully five hundred feet above it. It meant that they themselves could not see the sheep and men of course – but that did not matter, since there was nowhere else that they could go but down the Deadwater to the Tyne.

Presently they could see the road quite clearly, snaking down the broad valley away in front of them, beside the thin line of the railway and the sparkling river. They could see where the road crossed the Deadwater, too – but there were no lorries there. There was nothing like a lorry or a car to be seen in all the wide spread of land below them. Nor a house, either. The sun was just rising above the tall hills behind them.

Ken frowned. It looked as though he had thought wrong, somehow. And yet – what other answer could there be? He jutted his chin stubbornly.

'I still think they're thieves,' he said. 'Maybe the lorries are to meet them – and aren't there yet.'

46

Fiona did not argue with him. She would be quite glad to get down to that nice safe road, thieves or none.

The Deadwater's glen broadened and opened out as it neared the larger valley, so that the two young people had to keep farther and farther back to prevent themselves from being visible from down there. They were less than a mile from the road when Ken suddenly reined up again.

'Look, Fiona!' he cried. 'See those trees? In the glen, there. I saw a bright flash in them just now.'

He was pointing to where, fully half a mile up from the road in the floor of the glen, there was a square plantation of trees, on the far side of the Deadwater Burn.

'A flash, Ken? I didn't see anything. What on earth could that be?'

Ken turned Demon round, and moved back on their tracks a few paces.

'It might have been . . . Yes – there it is again. See? It's the slanting sunlight catching on something in that wood. Glass, I expect. See – there's two of them. Two gleams. There's no windows in there – no house.'

'Yes, I see now. Do you think . . . ?'

'Of course. It's lorries. They've got them parked

47

in there. Hidden. They've brought them up the burnside, away from the road. There's a grassy Roman road crossing slantwise down there, to join the Catrail. This whole area's criss-crossed with Roman roads. That would help them to get so far up. The rest of the way they'd just have to run over the grass. Well – satisfied now? Nobody who has any right to be there would bring their lorries all that way over difficult ground, and hide them deep in a wood!'

'No – that's true,' agreed Fiona. 'You must be right. What do we do now?'

Ken was biting his lip. 'I wish . . . if we could only keep those lorries from getting out again. Out of the wood – or back on to the road, anyway. How could we do it?'

'There wouldn't be any gate that we could shut – jam shut, so that they couldn't get through? Or wall that we could break down, to block the way . . .?'

'Nothing that *we* could do, that six big husky men couldn't *undo*, a lot more easily! That's the trouble. And we haven't so very long. I mean, even at the rate they're going, they'll be down to that wood in . . . well, it's maybe a mile and a half. Say in three-quarters of an hour. No time for us to get to the road, find somewhere with a telephone, and get police or somebody to come all the way up here – out of their beds. These thieves would be well away long before that.'

'They've got to load the sheep on to the lorries,' Fiona reminded him. 'That will take a while.'

'Not very long – even if they're not expert at it. Ten minutes or so. I wonder . . . I wonder if they've left a guard on the lorries themselves?'

'Oh, my goodness me! You think we should do something to them? Risk doing that? Let out the air from the tyres, or something?'

'I think I could do better than that!' Ken said. 'But there may be men there, watching them.'

'There may not even be lorries there, Ken,' the girl pointed out. 'It's just a guess, after all. We can only be sure that there is glass in there, reflecting the sun. That's all.'

'I'll bet my boots they're lorries!' the boy answered. 'But there's only one way to make sure – and that's to go and see, but without being seen ourselves. And that means we'll have to hurry. Come on, Fiona!'

CHAPTER FIVE

Ken Hits Back

THEY rode back, over the skyline from the glen, and then went as fast as Fiona dared over the broken ground downhill to the road. Up its firm tarmacadam surface they clattered at a canter.

When the Deadwater valley began to open on their right, they found a gate in the drystone wall, and passed through. They rode as far as they could risk, up into the mouth of the glen. Fortunately there were other small plantations of trees between that top one and the road to offer them cover.

At length they halted in a scattering of thorn-trees and gorse-bushes, as far up as they dared go. The plantation where they had seen the gleams of light was on the other side of the burn, and about four hundred yards farther up still. They peered up the glen, blinking in the dazzle of the early morning sunlight that came pouring down it from the east. The sheep and herders were still invisible from here.

'Can't take the horses farther,' Ken told the girl. 'I'm going forward on foot. Plenty of cover, if I keep low. You wait here, with the horses.'

'What are you going to do, Ken?' They were both whispering, though there could be no need for that.

'Depends what I find. If there's nobody there, I'll do what I can with the lorries. If I need help, I'll come to the edge of the trees and wave for you. If there *is* a guard – well, I suppose we'll just have to think of something else. Okay?'

'All right. But . . . be careful, Ken!'

He left her, and went forward on foot, cautiously, but wasting no time. The burn had dug a deep channel for itself in the winter spates, and since it was no more than half-full now, he was able to slip down into this and use it as a covered route to take him onwards. It brought him quite close to the plantation. As he left the burnside and went at a crouching run across the open ground between, he noticed the tracks of heavy tyres on the turf and mud. His guess had not been so far out then!

In the shelter of the trees Ken moved slowly, quietly, so as not to make any noise of breaking twigs. And soon, through the branches, he saw what he was seeking – three large high-sided lorries, double-decked to take two layers of sheep on each, drawn up close together in a grassy glade.

The boy stared. He could see no sign of a man about – from this side, at any rate. He would work round to the other side, and look from there.

As he went soundlessly, he noticed that none of the lorries had any names painted on them.

At the far side, there was still nobody to be seen. Everything was quiet – except for his heart, which was thumping a little from more than hurrying. Ken stepped out into the open glade.

He looked at the lorries. They seemed awfully big, somehow. He knew how to make a car's engine useless – immobilizing it, it was called – by taking away a small part called the rotor from the electrical system. He supposed that lorries would be just the same – but they did look so much more powerful and impressive. Plucking up his courage, he was just going to start lifting the bonnet of the first one when it occurred to him that it probably would be best to do the last one first – just in case he couldn't manage them all in the time. Then the front ones would have a job getting past the last one, for the glade was very narrow, and it would be difficult to push such a large and heavy vehicle out of the way.

Ken was just going up to the bonnet of the third lorry when he got a shock. There was a man sitting inside the cab. For a moment the boy was rooted to the spot in panic – and then he realized that the man was asleep, his mouth slightly open.

On tiptoe Ken crept back into the cover of the trees again.

He bit his lip. He had not been seen – but he certainly could not go lifting the bonnets of lorries with that man there. What on earth was he to do now?

After a few moments he hurried back to the edge of the wood, and peered up the glen. Still there was no sign of the sheep – the valley made a bend less than half a mile up, and there was no knowing how close they were beyond that. Not bothering to crouch this time, he ran out and over to the burn again, to retrace his steps to where he had left Fiona.

'There's a man sleeping in one of the lorries,' he panted out to her. 'Yes – there are lorries there. Three of them. But I can't do anything to them with

53

that chap there. I'm wondering if we can't get him away somehow?'

'How could we do that, Ken?'

'Well, I wonder if we could decoy him away, just for a little – to give me time to get under the bonnets of the lorries. It would mean *you* decoying him, I'm afraid. Suppose you came into the wood with me, and showed yourself – so that the man saw you? And then ran away. He'd follow you, for sure. He'd be worried that you'd go and tell somebody else what you'd seen. How fast can you run, Fiona?'

'As fast as you, I'm sure – or nearly,' she said stoutly.

'Faster than a grown-up man?'

'I should think so. *As* fast, anyway. At least till I got back to the horses here. Then I could just ride away from him, couldn't I?'

'No – that wouldn't do. That wouldn't take long enough. I mean, it would only take two or three minutes for you, and him, to get this far. He wouldn't chase on after you, on a horse. So he'd turn back. It wouldn't give me time enough to do anything to all three lorries.'

'Well, I'd just have to keep running then. On foot. Up the hill, say. I'd be quicker up the hillside than a big heavy man, I'm sure. I'll do that, Ken.'

He frowned. 'I'm not awfully keen on this, you know,' he said. 'I mean, getting you mixed up in something that might be dangerous. I don't think my people would be very pleased . . .'

'Goodness – what nonsense! It's a bit late to think about that now, isn't it, anyway? Of course I'll do it. It won't be dangerous, anyway. They wouldn't hurt me, if they did catch me – which they won't. They might hold me, till they got away with their lorries – but I'm sure they wouldn't hurt me. Why should they?'

'M'mmm. Well – I can't think of anything else. And we haven't much time, or the people with the sheep will be here . . .'

'Come on, then,' Fiona urged. 'We'll tie the horses to trees here, and I'll run *away* from this direction. Later, I mean. Up the hill where we were before. Then, when you've finished at the lorries, you can come back here for the horses, and bring them round the way we've just come, to meet me on the hill. Will that do?'

'Good for you, Fiona!' the boy said admiringly. 'For a girl, you're not bad, you know! But I hope that man's no sprinter!'

Leaving the horses, they crept forward together, by the same route that Ken had taken before. In the

55

wood all was as it had been. The man still slept in his cab. But Ken thought that he could hear baaing on the air.

'Right,' he whispered. 'If you go out in front, there – show yourself. You will have to make a noise of some sort, to wake him up, to attract his attention. Sing or something. Then bolt, but not before you see he's going to come after you. I think he will.'

'But if he doesn't, Ken?'

'Well, you'll have to work him up, somehow. You might climb up on to the front lorry, and start hooting the horn. That would make him mad, surely?'

'Mercy! I'd look an awful ass doing that!'

'What does that matter? The thing is to get him chasing after you. He certainly wouldn't want a lot of horn-blowing, giving away that there were lorries hidden in here. He couldn't be sure that there was nobody else about to hear. After all, where had *you* come from?'

'All right. I'll do it. I hope you manage with the lorries.'

'Yes. Good luck, Fiona. And don't let him catch you, for any sake! If you do need help – if you were to fall, or anything – shout for me. I'd hear you, and come. He looks an oldish man, so I don't think he'll be able to run fast.'

56

'I hope we're not being terrible idiots, Ken . . .?'

'Of course not. We've got to do something – and what else is there to do? Off you go, then.' He squeezed her arm. 'I'll keep hidden till I see what happens.'

Fiona crept off, still in the cover of the trees. She moved on until she was thirty or forty yards in front of the first lorry, and very near the far edge of the wood. Then she stepped out into the open glade. She stood for a few moments, looking back uncertainly – obviously trying to see whether the man in the last lorry was awake yet. Ken, from his hiding-place, could see that he still slept. Then, her hands thrust into the pockets of her borrowed breeches, the girl began to stroll forwards. And her voice rose in song, high and clear, a good Highland song – *Ho-Ro My Nut-Brown Maiden.*

The man in the lorry cannot have been very deeply asleep, for he woke up at once, leaning forward in the cab, and peering. Fiona came on, her voice a little unsteady perhaps. Ken hoped that the man would not just sit still.

He did not. Opening the door of his cab, he jumped down, and stood looking at the girl.

Fiona played up very well. She acted as though she had just seen the man. She stopped dead in her

tracks. She stopped singing, too. Then, as he took a
step towards her, she glanced from side to side, as
though in sudden panic, and after a moment or two
of hesitation, she turned and took to her heels, running off into the trees to her left, southwards.

'Hey, you!' the lorry-driver shouted. 'Stop it! Here – come back. Come here, you!'

Fiona ran on the faster, dodging among the trees. Cursing, the man began to run after her, his heavy tread making a great crackling and trampling in the dead twigs and undergrowth. He bawled after the girl for a few moments – and then evidently decided to save his breath for running.

Ken was wildly excited. He would have liked to follow on, at least to the edge of the plantation, to see how the chase went. But time was precious – that was the whole point of Fiona's effort. The man might get discouraged very quickly, give up the chase, and come back after only a minute or two. As he saw the fellow disappear among the trees and bushes, Ken darted quickly out of his hiding, crouching low, and ran to the front of the third lorry.

Fumbling a little in his excitement, he unhooked the catches that held the bonnet shut. It opened from the top, not the bottom. Thrusting it aside, he peered in at the great, dirty, old-fashioned engine. It was very different from the car engines that he knew, but he was quite used to working with his father's farm tractors, and the electrical system was not unlike theirs. Anyway, the bunched rubber leads from the sparking-plugs showed him where to

59

look for his rotor under the distributor-head. Snapping back the clips, he uncovered it, and whisked out the small but vital piece of mechanism and put it into his pocket. Without it, the only way that lorry would move was by being pushed or towed.

Ken tried to fix the lid of the bonnet properly in place, but found it awkward. His ears all the while seemed to be stretching out, listening for the return of that man. He decided that it was more important to get the other lorries dealt with first, and to leave the covering up till later, if he was given the time. He ran on to the next truck.

This one was a slightly more modern model, and he wasted precious moments hunting for the catch that held down the bonnet-cover. But when he found it at the front, and pressed down a little lever, the lid lifted up much more easily and conveniently. The engine was different too, but again the rubber leads guided him to the part that he wanted. In a few seconds the rotor of this one was in his pocket also. Moreover, the bonnet-cover had only to be pulled down, and it clicked satisfactorily shut of its own accord. Nobody would suspect anything wrong here till the self-starter refused to work.

As he ran to the front lorry, Ken paused to listen. From the angry shouting in the distance he gathered, to his relief, that the man had stopped trying to catch Fiona, and was contenting himself with threats. He could hear nothing else but the pounding of his own heart, a faint stir of wind among the tree-tops, and, clearer now, the baaing of many sheep.

Hastily he went to work on this last truck. He did not have to open the bonnet here, for the side of the cover was already leaning open. Presumably the long climb up to the Deadwater had overheated the engine, and the driver had opened it up to let cool air in, and forgotten to close it again. So this one, another old vehicle, was the simplest of all to deal with. Ken put the third rotor into that pocket of his.

Then he hurried back to the lorry that he had tackled first, and after a bit of tugging, managed to fix one of the catches that held down the bonnet – though nothing that he could do would make the other shut properly. Still there was no sound.

61

Picking his way as fast as he could, without making a noise, the boy made for the edge of the wood, some distance farther down than the point where Fiona had led the lorry-driver out. As soon as he could see what was going on, he stopped. The scene was perfectly clear. Across the burn – which Fiona and her pursuer must have splashed over – the hillside rose, not very steeply, up through young, pale-green bracken and gorse-bushes to the deer-hair grass of the higher ground. Up there he could see Fiona still climbing, though not running any more, and occasionally stooping to use her hands to help herself up. She looked puffed, but still game and going strong. The lorry-driver looked puffed too – and he was not going strong. He was coming back, downhill, heavily, shoulders hunched, an angry and breathless man.

Ken almost cheered. Good old Fiona!

Though the returning man did not seem to be looking at anything else but where to put his feet, Ken waited until the fellow was safely back into the cover of the plantation before he himself slipped out at the bottom end, and over into the burn-channel. In a couple of minutes he was back at the horses, leading them quietly out towards the road.

CHAPTER SIX

Trailing Trouble

KEN finished the last lap of his ride round and up
the hill almost at a gallop, poor Walter Scott having
to pound along willy-nilly behind the dashing and
longer-legged Demon, his empty stirrups flap-
flapping against his round sides.

'Grand! Splendid!' the boy cried to Fiona, who
had been visible for quite a while, sitting on a
boulder, just over the brow of the hill from the
Deadwater valley. 'You did that beautifully. Look!'
He put his hand into his pocket and brought out the
three rotors.

'Goodness! Is that all they are? Just those wee
things!' she wondered.

'Their size isn't important. It's what they do.
Without them, no electric current, no life, reaches
the engine.'

'Then they can't move? The lorries are all stuck
there? They wouldn't carry spare ones – whatever
you call them?'

'I shouldn't think so. I've never heard of anybody

63

doing that. They are not things that can break down, or go wrong, you see. Only if they are deliberately taken away. No – they're stuck, all right, for the time being.'

'What happens next, then?'

'Well, I haven't just thought it out properly yet. It sort of depends on what the *thieves* do now. We want to catch them properly – not just prevent them getting away with this haul of sheep. If we can.'

'Of course,' Fiona agreed. 'But if they can't get away, we've time to go and get help now.'

'Yes. But it's not quite so simple as that. It all depends what they do when they find that they can't move their lorries. They're not just going to sit down beside them and wait for trouble. They may bolt in a bunch, or scatter into the hills.'

'And just leave their lorries? Wouldn't that be a terrible loss to them? Surely they're not likely to do that?' asked Fiona.

'What else can they do? Anyway, they may well have stolen the lorries in the first place. That's often done, I believe. Did you notice that the names of the owners had been painted out?' said Ken, frowning. 'They might send one or two of them to thumb a lift on the road, of course. Down to the nearest garage, to try to get other rotors; but that would take a good long time. They'd have to go to some big garage – no small place would be likely to have a lot of these parts, to fit three different kinds of lorry. Bellingham's the nearest village – but I don't think there would be a big enough garage there. That's on the English side, about fifteen miles away. Hexham would be the nearest town of any size, that side. That's twice as far. Nearer to Hawick or Jedburgh, on our own side. Twenty miles, by road, each.'

He looked at his watch. It was six-fifteen. 'Even if they were very lucky with lifts, they couldn't be back here in under two hours, at least. More, probably. They'd have a job finding a garage open at this time of day.'

'They'd know that whoever pinched their what-you-call-thems could have got help brought up by then, surely?' Fiona suggested.

'Well – it's not so easy for us to do that either, you know. I mean, to get help up here. We're in about as lonely a bit of Britain as there is, south of your High-lands. And it's no use just getting one or two men to help, if we're to catch this lot. We need a big bunch.'

'The police. We should find a phone, and tell the police . . .'

'Where? The nearest policemen will be in Bellingham – but they'll be only a couple of country bobbies, on bikes. We'd have as much trouble getting a strong force of police up here, as these thieves would getting rotors! This is England, too, remember – Scots police wouldn't do. They would have to come from Hexham, over twenty-five miles away – that is, if we could convince them of what has happened, just by talking over the phone.'

'Mercy on us – what a business!' Fiona sighed gustily. 'We'll just have to go and try to find the farmer – the owner of these sheep. Let him do the rest, Ken.'

'Maybe.' Ken did not sound enthusiastic. 'I'd hate to see these people get away with it now, after what we've done, when we've a chance to catch them red-handed. *We* lost some sheep about five months ago. The police couldn't do anything for us. We never heard any more about it. Probably these are the same folk.' He shrugged. 'Let's go up to the ridge, and look over – see what they're doing, at least.'

Leaving the horses safely out of sight, they crept up to the skyline and far enough over to look down into the Deadwater valley. They lay flat, watching.

So far the only commotion was that of agitated sheep. Quite a lot of these were hemmed in by dogs and a couple of men around the top end of the plantation. Other beasts could be seen among the trees. Obviously the loading-up process was still going on, which meant, presumably, that nobody had yet discovered that the lorries had been interfered with.

As they watched, and time passed, Ken said, 'They're taking much longer about loading than I'd expected. They've got a lot of beasts there, of course. It's hard to count, at this distance, but I'd say there are between forty and fifty left outside the wood still. How many they have all together, I don't know. But three double-decked lorries that size would be able to carry forty or more each. So they could have aimed at stealing a hundred and twenty or so, at least. At six to eight pounds apiece, that's quite a haul.'

'Heavens, that could be nearly a thousand pounds!' exclaimed Fiona. 'I'd no idea that there was anything like that in it.'

'Oh, yes. They do things in a big way. But they're not very good at loading sheep on to trucks. We could teach them a thing or two about that.'

It was after seven before the last of the sheep had disappeared into the wood, and the men and dogs with them. There was another spell of waiting. Ken was fretting with impatience.

'It seems terrible, lying here doing nothing,' he said. 'But until we've got some idea what *they* mean to do, there's not much that we can do ourselves.'

But after a bit their waiting was rewarded. Men came bursting out from the edge of the plantation, staring this way and that. One man was pointing up-hill, almost directly towards where they lay hidden – no doubt the hero whom Fiona had outrun. The young people wondered what sort of story he was telling the others. Obviously the robbers had discovered how they had been tricked.

'D'you think they'll come up here, after us?' Fiona asked. 'They won't know we've got horses.'

'We just can't tell. They might. I don't think so though. They'll probably reckon that we've had too long a start.'

The men below them seemed to be holding a council-of-war, standing together in a huddle at the edge of the trees, one or the other occasionally waving an arm. After a while they all turned and went back into the wood.

'I think we ought to go down to the road and stop a car,' Fiona suggested. 'At least get *some* message out for help. Let *somebody* know what's going on.'

'I know how you feel,' Ken told her, 'but I don't see what good that's going to do. Not till we've an

68

idea what *they'll* do next. Better to keep an eye on them, from up here. And, anyway, I've been glancing at the road all the time, and I haven't seen a single car this morning.'

They went on arguing about it, Fiona saying she at least should go for help and Ken doubting whether she could get it in time to be of any use, when their minds were made up for them and they got the clue that they were waiting for. It was not in the least what they had expected.

Sheep began to issue out from that plantation again, at the same top end where they had been driven in: sheep on their own feet – lots of sheep. Behind them came the men and dogs, just as before – only going in the opposite direction this time.

'Well, I'm blowed!' Ken cried. 'Look at that. Going back again – the lot of them!'

'They're giving up! We've beaten them!' Fiona said gleefully. 'We've won, Ken. They're going to return those sheep where they got them . . . aren't they?'

The boy was frowning doubtfully.

'I'm not so sure about that,' he said. 'In fact, I don't think they'll do that. Why should they, after all? They don't care a hang about the sheep, or the farmer's convenience. If they were just packing up, accepting defeat and clearing out, they'd just leave the sheep where they were and bolt. They'd never go to the bother of taking them back where they got them. No – they've something else in mind, I think.'

'But, Ken, if they can't move their lorries from there, then just to leave all those sheep roaming about would draw attention to the lorries, wouldn't it? That's may be why they're driving the sheep away a bit. Maybe they're only going to take them round

70

the bend in the glen, and out of sight. Leave them there?'

'That's possible, I suppose. We'll soon know. But you wouldn't think it would take all those men to do that – four of them. They've left two more men behind – there were six herding before. That's three still at the lorries. I wonder . . .?'

As the sheep and men moved slowly up the glen, and round the bend out of sight, the young people rose up, collected their horses, and moved on eastwards too, parallel with the others behind the crest of the hill. After a bit, they dismounted, and crept up to the ridge again, farther up.

The shepherding was still going on. In a long straggling line the sheep were moving on steadily up the glen, baaing loud protest again. They had not been left just around the bend.

For a while Ken and Fiona watched, till it was quite clear that, whatever they meant to do, the thieves were not leaving the sheep and hurrying back to the lorries. The youngsters were puzzled.

'What does it mean, Ken?' Fiona asked. 'Where are they going?'

'There's only the one answer, I think,' the boy said. 'They're not going to leave go of the best part of a thousand pounds so easily! They're going to

drive those sheep deep into the hills and out by some
other route. That must be it. Those other two they've
left behind will probably go down to the road and
thumb a lift to try and get new rotors. Then they
can come back and get the lorries out of there, and
take them to some new meeting-place. That's why
they've left three drivers. There's no crime in just
parking lorries off the road, so nobody'll be able to
stop them. They'll have all day for it – plenty of time,
for it's miles and miles to any other road. I mean,
the sheep will have to be driven a long, long way to
get them to anywhere else that lorries can reach.
There's a hundred and fifty square miles of empty
roadless hill ahead of them, there!'

'Oh, dear!' Fiona's sigh was almost a groan. 'So
it's no good? After all we've done, they're going to
get away, after all!'

'Not if I can help it!' Ken said determinedly.
'There must be some way of stopping them. If
I could only think . . .'

'But how can there be? After all, if it was going to
be difficult getting help here near the road, how on
earth can we get people to chase them deep into
these hills? They'll soon be away, lost to us. We can't
go following them for ever – and you said yourself
that these hills are absolutely empty.'

'Empty . . .!' Ken repeated the word slowly – and then turned to her, his eyes shining. 'Of course! By Jove – why didn't I think of that before? They're empty, yes. Usually. But not to-day. To-day's the Rulekirk Common Riding! There'll be lashings of people – a great cavalcade of horsemen, up on the Cheviot ridge to-day. The only day in the whole year when there is! If we could get them . . .'

'But when?' Fiona asked, with despair in her voice. 'They won't be up here for ages yet, will they? And only up to the Border-line, didn't you say? By that time, these wretched thieves will be miles away, lost among the hills.'

'Listen,' Ken said, more or less thinking aloud. 'The cavalcade is due up on the Peel Fell ridge there at 10.30. They have the Provost's Breakfast and a speech or two, and then leave Rulekirk at 8.30, getting up here two hours later. That's in an hour and a quarter now. There'll be a lot of them. Up to a hundred. Plenty to split up into a few big parties, to hunt through the hills. If we were to meet them up there . . . ?'

'D'you think they'd do it, Ken? I mean, give up whatever they do, the official sort of programme, and start hunting sheep-stealers instead?'

'I don't know – but it's worth a try. Some would, surely. Are you game, Fiona?'

'Well – yes. But it'll take a long time. And . . . I'm awfully hungry, Ken!'

'So am I. We've a sandwich each left, and some biscuits. We'll have them now. As well we saved them. And drink a lot of burn-water – that helps to fill your tummy up. But it's a chance, isn't it? Worth taking?'

'Yes. Yes. How long will it take us to get to this place? Where the riders come?'

'Oh, not very long. From here, less than an hour, on horseback. No hurry about that – we've three hours. We'd better trail on behind the thieves, keeping well out of sight. See which way they go. Then up to the Peel Fell ridge later. Okay?'

'Yes. Let's have that sandwich, shall we?'

'Look,' Ken pointed. Away down at the road, three figures had appeared, only just visible from here. They began to walk down the road eastwards. The English side. Munching, the youngsters watched them go.

'I wish we could eat grass and bracken shoots – like the horses,' the hungry Fiona said.

CHAPTER SEVEN

Parting Company

Mile after slow mile they trailed that flock of sheep, keeping well back and out of sight. It was weary, dull work, but not difficult, because the herdsmen kept to the low ground as far as possible, and the young people were able to remain high up where they were not readily seen from below. But it was terribly tiresome to have to creep along at the pace of a flock of sheep – tired and grumbling sheep at that.

Both the boy and the girl were hungrier than they could ever remember having been before. They had eaten the last crumbs out of their paper bags, and they drank from every clean-looking burn that

75

they passed. They led their horses on foot most of the way.

The sheep did not travel at more than two miles an hour. Their herders drove them away from the Deadwater about three miles up, where it had become just a narrow, tinkling rill, and struck off over soft, boggy ground to the beginnings of another valley. From this they branched off into a third, ever deeper into the hills, but the general direction was south by east. Ken became fairly sure that the men intended to work gradually round and down to the Tyne road again, much lower down.

At length, with the youngsters up on the brow of a long rounded hill where they could go no farther for quite a while without being very visible from the valley below, Ken drew up. He looked from his watch to the distant, straggling flock of sheep. They were certainly getting farther and farther from Peel Fell.

'This won't do, Fiona,' he said. 'It's nine-thirty. The riders will be up on the ridge of Peel Fell in an hour. It's going to take us all our time to get there by then. We can't keep trailing on and on like this.'

'But look, Ken!' Fiona waved her hand at all the great sea of hill and valley that stretched seemingly without end before them. 'Once we lose them in there, we'll never find them again. This place is an absolute maze!'

'I know. It will be difficult. But what can we do?' asked Ken.

'We'll have to split up,' the girl said, decidedly. 'One of us will have to keep on after them. The other must go and fetch your Common Riders.'

Ken glanced at her, sideways. This had been in his own mind for quite some time, but he had not dared to suggest it to her. Certainly it would be the most useful thing to do, but it was not a very nice thought, to leave a girl alone in these desolate hills that she did not know – especially as there could not be much question as to who should do what.

'*You* don't know the way to Peel Fell from here,' he pointed out. 'I don't, myself – but I can find it.'

'Yes,' she nodded. 'It will have to be you that goes for help, and me that follows on after the thieves.'

'But . . . will you do that, Fiona? All alone? I mean – it's not a very nice job for you, is it?'

'Of course I'll do it. Somebody's got to do it, if we're going to stop these people and catch them red-handed. I'll be all right. I'll just go on doing what we've been doing. I'll keep them in sight – but keep well out of their way.'

'It's a pretty decent thing to do,' Ken said admiringly. 'Not many girls would offer to take on a job like that, alone . . .'

'Oh, don't be silly,' Fiona told him. 'I'm enjoying it. If only my tummy wasn't so empty! The only thing is – you – you don't think that mist would come down again? Like it did yesterday? I would hate to be lost in it again, all alone.'

Ken looked about him, and shook his head.

'I shouldn't think so. It's much fresher than it was yesterday. Not the same sort of weather at all. That was unusual, you know. I'm pretty sure that it will stay clear to-day. Until evening, at any rate.'

'That's fine, then. The only question now is – how are you to find *me*, when you come back with the others? I mean, I won't be very easy to pick out either, even if I do keep up on higher ground, in all this jumble of hills.'

'No. But I think I know the way out of that difficulty. Smoke. Like the Red Indians used for signalling. Smoke signals. Here are the matches. What you have to do is to ride up to the top of the nearest hill to where you are, just after ten-thirty, and light a fire of dead grass and old heather. It will set up a big column of smoke, especially the grass. We'll see it for miles on a clear day like this. Do it on a bare

78

patch, so that it doesn't start a hill fire. We'll ride in that direction.'

'That's a jolly good idea! I'd better take all the paper we've got. It's not much.'

'You'll find, using the fuzzy tops of dead heather to start it, that you won't need paper. I didn't use any last night, even when everything was dampish. You may have to make more than the one fire. After all it will take us well over an hour to reach you, once I get the others going. We'll probably need guiding farther.'

'All right,' said Fiona, then added anxiously. 'But, Ken – won't the thieves see the smoke signals too?'

'I expect they will. That can't be helped. But, even if they realize it's to do with them, what can they do about it? They won't take it very seriously, I shouldn't think. Probably think it's Boy Scouts or something. After all, they're not likely to know that there are many people to be brought down on them. They won't know about the Rulekirk riders coming up, I don't suppose.'

'That's true. Well – is there anything else? For it's time you were away, isn't it?'

'It *is* time, yes. No – I can't think of anything else. I don't see that these thieves can be of any danger to you, Fiona. You've got a horse and they haven't.

They can't chase you, even if they see you. You should be all right. Don't worry about anything. I'll be back with you in between two and three hours. I'll come for you, of course, whatever happens – I mean, even if none of the Common Riding people believe me, or will come back with me. But they *will* come, of course. Okay?'

'Yes. Right-ho, Ken. Come back soon. I . . . I'll look forward to seeing you again.' Fiona's voice sounded a little bit trembly.

'Keep your chin up!' he told her, grinning. 'This is as good as marooning those salmon-poachers on Spaniards' Isle last year! See you about noon. Up, the MacBrides!'

And Ken turned Demon's black head round, and set off northwards, digging in his heels. He looked back after a couple of hundred yards to wave. Fiona MacBride and Walter Scott looked very small and lonely, somehow, alone against the tremendous background of the Cheviots.

CHAPTER EIGHT

Most Uncommon Riding

KEN rode hard, giving Demon his head as much as he dared over the broken, uneven ground. Direction was not difficult, for it was easy to tell the north from the position of the sun. He kept riding in that direction until he topped a ridge high enough for an extensive view, and there, three or four miles away ahead of him, was the unmistakable outline of Peel Fell.

Reaching that high hill was not so simple as finding it, of course. There were many deep valleys to cross, streams to jump or ford, slopes to climb, and treacherous peat-bogs to work round. But Demon was strong and spirited, trained to rough ground, and glad to have his head after all that slow trailing after sheep. The difficult miles shortened under pounding hooves.

At last the main ridge was clear before them, and Demon, froth-spattered, put his head down to the long climb gallantly. It was quarter-past ten.

Dead on the stroke of ten-thirty, Ken rode up on to the crest of the wide summit ridge, and the Border-line. The great stone that marked the site of the famous Rescue of Rulehead Rab rose before him. He was first on the scene, at any rate.

He urged his black on a little farther, over the brow of the ridge to where he could look down the long northern slopes beyond, into Scotland. And there, only a few hundred yards below him, three riders bunched together, the centre man in a vivid red coat and blue bonnet, spurred their sweating horses upwards. Behind, fully half a mile behind, a single horseman rode, a large banner fluttering proudly above him in the breeze; and beyond him, at a respectful distance, followed a great company scattered far and wide over the face of the hillside – the Rulekirk Cornet and his cavalcade of supporters.

Ken, in spite of all that was on his mind, felt a thrill of excitement and pride at the sight, at the colour and vigour and action of it all.

The three nearmost horsemen came thundering up in grand style, scattering turf from flying hooves. It was the Common Riding Marshal and his two assistants, whose duty was to clear the way for the Cornet and the Flag, and to see that the whole programme was kept up to time and in order. Ken knew the Marshal – he was a butcher in the town.

Ken waved, and grinned.

'Hullo!' he shouted. 'I'm jolly glad to see you, Mr Kerr.'

But there was no answering smile from the Marshal, as he pulled up his big roan horse almost on to its hind quarters.

'Hi – oot o' the way there, boy!' he cried, frowning, with a sweep of his arm as though he would wipe Ken off the scene. 'Whit d'you think you're doing here, eh? You ken weel enough naebody's allowed to ride in front o' the Marshal and the Cornet.'

'Oh, I know that, yes. But this is different, you see. I didn't . . .'

'It's no' different, boy! Oot o' the way, noo! Take yoursel' and your horse away to the side, there. Oot o' sight. Quick, noo – off wi' you! I'm right ashamed o' you, young Rutherford!'

'But, Mr Kerr – this is important! I didn't come riding in front of anybody . . .'

'Wheesht, boy! I've nae time for your blethers, the noo. Off wi' you.' And the Marshal pulled round his beast, its forelegs pawing the air, and put a horn to his lips to blow a long, strong, double blast that echoed and re-echoed around the hills. One of his assistants waved Ken curtly away.

Biting his lip, and trying hard to keep his face from showing how bitter and upset he felt, the boy turned Demon round and rode slowly away. He had never imagined anything like this. It was perfectly true, of course, that one of the things that just was not done was for any rider to get in front of the Cornet and the Colours, except for the Marshal himself. He recognized that it would look as though he had ridden up here, ahead of the cavalcade, in order to be first on the scene, to steal a march on everybody else and get himself noticed. But surely they knew that he would never do a thing like that, brought up in the Common Riding tradition as he was? The Marshal might at least have listened to him.

But the Marshal had other things to think about. He was sounding his horn, right and left, and waving his assistants out on to the flanks, a man with a lot on his mind – for the Cornet's programme was a big one, and had to be timed most carefully; otherwise everything would be in a fearful muddle by the end of it.

Ken drew up three hundred yards away, and turned to sit his horse and watch, impatiently.

The Cornet was coming near now, a splendid figure in dark green coat, white breeches and gleaming knee-boots, a top-hat on his head and the town's sash across his chest, ribboned rosettes fluttering from his lapel and from the top of the streaming banner that he held up as though on a lance. The cornets of the two years before had now spurred up to close behind him, his Right and Left as they were called, dressed as he was, without the sash of honour. To-day, the Rulekirk Cornet was King of the Borderland – though the cornets and callants of all the other Scots Border burghs were riding in his cavalcade behind. He was riding grandly, Ken had to admit, coming up the hill at an all-out gallop, on a magnificent grey with flaring nostrils, outstretched head, and streaming mane. That big flapping banner on its pole was a mighty difficult thing to carry and control at the gallop, Ken knew well. A lump rose in the boy's throat at the sight, as always. It was Ken's ambition to be Cornet himself some day.

With a great clatter these three pounded up, pulling up their snorting horses whose hooves scored long red scars in the green turf. The Cornet jumped down, and helped by his Right and Left, climbed up on to the top of the massive stone, holding the banner high. The first of the great cavalcade came dashing up, and the whole hillside shook with the pounding and drumming of hundreds of hooves. Scores and scores of riders reined in, young and old, men and women, flushed and breathless, mud- and foam-splattered, some dirty from tumbles, all excited and shouting. The Marshal's horn blared out again for silence, and the Cornet led the cheers for Rulekirk and the Colours, waving the silken banner in the breeze. Then the stirring Common Riding song rang out, and everybody joined in.

Ken rode forward now. He had great difficulty in pressing through the throng, trying to get close to the leaders. He was just one boy amongst a hundred now, and nobody paid the least attention to him. He dismounted, leaving Demon loose, among the other horses. He was making for Rulekirk's Provost, a friend of his father's, who was in the centre of a laughing party.

But Ken just could not get to him. There were too many riders and horses and guests in the way – even reporters and photographers, all wanting to reach the important people. Folk frowned at the pushing boy, thinking him cheeky and bad-mannered. Nobody would listen to his demands that he must talk

86

to the Provost or the Marshal or somebody in charge of things.

Then his arm was grabbed. It was a neighbouring farmer.

'Ken,' this man exclaimed. 'Where did *you* spring from? I thought you were lost. Where did you get to last night? Your father was worried about you. How come you're here now . . .?'

'Oh, we were caught in the mist, Mr Scott. Couldn't find our way down,' Ken cried. 'But I'll tell you all that later. I must see the Provost first. Can you not help me? I can't get near him . . .'

'It wasn't very fair of you, Ken, to come on here this morning, without letting your people know. Was it?' the other went on. 'I saw your mother before I came away. She was very anxious about you. I think you should go right home, now . . .'

'No, no. Not just now. I must see the Provost. There's sheep-stealers to catch. It's important, Mr Scott. Won't you help me? Please . . .'

But the farmer, shrugging, had turned to speak to somebody else in the crush.

Unhappily Ken stared about him. This was terrible! Who would have thought it would have worked out like this? He would try to get to the Cornet. He was young, and might listen to him.

But the Cornet was the centre of an admiring throng, especially of giggling young women, and though Ken got fairly near him, and shouted his name, nobody heard him in all the shouting and laughter – or at least, paid any attention. He was just considering diving down amongst and between people's legs in an attempt to get closer, when the Marshal's horn rang out once more. The Provost was up on the top of the flat stone now, and helping another older man up: General Sir Patrick Home, who was now going to make the Rescue Oration.

Ken groaned. A speech, now! That might go on for ages and ages!

The General waited for the clapping to stop, cleared his throat, stroked his white moustaches, and began to speak. He had only got a few words out, when another voice rose high, to interrupt him.

'I say – please listen to *me!*' Ken cried, his voice cracking, and sounding horribly thin and squeaky somehow. 'It's terribly important. Really it is . . .'

There was a great growling and spluttering and shushing from all around him. People turned and frowned blackly at him, muttering to him to be quiet, to remember his manners. Somebody even grabbed his shoulder. It was one of the Marshal's assistants, standing nearby.

88

Ken twisted free, and darted off amongst the crowd again, pushing and wriggling. He was desperate now. He had to do *something*.

The General was just getting into his stride, after some hawing and humming, when right beneath him on the big stone Ken came climbing, scrambling to hoist himself up on hands and knees. Then he stood up there, before the entire shocked gathering, blinking hard, and clenching his fists to keep them from trembling.

The General's words faltered to a puffing close. He turned to stare at the interloper at his side.

'God bless my soul!' he said.

The angry murmur of the crowd grew into a roar.

'Please! Please!' Ken yelled. He clutched the General's arm. 'Please, sir – don't be angry. Let me speak – just for a moment. It means an awful lot. A girl – she's called Fiona – is needing help. Terribly. Please, sir!'

'Eh?' General Home had gone a slightly purple colour. He blinked. 'What's this, boy? A girl, d'you say? Needing help . . .?'

Ken could hardly hear him speak for the noise that the crowd was making. The Marshal and his assistants were pushing forward – obviously coming to remove him from the stone.

'Yes, sir,' he exclaimed. 'Help me, please. Make them listen to me – just for a little. Honest – I've got to get help for Fiona . . .'

The General made a hurrumphing sort of sound, loudly, and then raised his hand for silence. He had to stand like that for quite a few moments before he got it. Then he spoke.

'Mr Provost, Cornet Pringle, Ladies and Gentlemen – I'm not quite sure what all this is about. But this young man certainly seems to have something on his mind! It's about a lady too, I think – called Fiona apparently. Needing help. What we are to do about it, I'm not sure. But I think, probably, that the best and quickest thing to do is just to let him tell us about it, as briefly as he can – and then we maybe can get on with what we're here for.'

The crowd stirred. Everyone began to talk. Some people laughed – but most still looked angry.

'That's young Rutherford,' somebody shouted. 'Major Rutherford of Houndlaw's son.'

'Ken – I think you'd better get down. At once!' That was the Provost, speaking sternly. 'I don't know what's come over you.'

'I'll tell you,' Ken yelled, almost screamed. 'We've cornered a bunch of sheep-stealers. Over in the hills there. English side. Fiona MacBride and me. Fiona's still following them – and I came for help. For *your* help. If you come, we can catch them all, red-handed.'

'Goodness me! What on earth is the boy talking about?' the General gasped.

'Ken – are you crazy?' the Provost demanded. 'What nonsense is this . . .?'

'It's not nonsense – it's the truth, sir,' the boy cried. 'We were lost in the mist last night. Up here. In the early morning, we heard baaing. Lots of sheep. We made for the sound, and saw a flock being driven down. At four o'clock in the morning. There were six men, and dogs. Heading down the Deadwater. Making for the Tyne road. We were on horses, and went round ahead. We discovered three lorries hidden in a wood, near the road. I put the lorries out of action. So they couldn't get away on them. They had to turn back. They're heading through the hills again now, with Fiona trailing them, keeping them in sight. We've got to catch them. You all know how many sheep have been stolen. I knew you all would be coming up here. So I rode here for help. But Fiona's all alone . . .' Ken's voice broke.

'Mercy on us!' The Provost looked about him uncertainly. 'This is . . . this is fantastic! Are you really telling the truth, Ken?'

'Of course I am! D'you think I'd make up a thing like that? Look – here's the rotors I pinched from the three lorries!' And Ken held up the three small pieces of mechanism.

It was unlikely that anyone could see what was in the boy's hand. But it was extraordinary the effect that that gesture had on everyone. The naming of those essential car-parts, so humdrum and down-to-earth, seemed to make the whole business become real, practical, something to take seriously, all at once. Quite suddenly the crowd believed him – all because of the rotors. Every man there knew that to remove these parts was the surest and simplest way to cripple any motor vehicle.

There was a great shouting of questions now, everybody speaking at once.

Ken was almost jumping up and down on that stone, because he was unable now to make himself heard for the noise. Suddenly somebody else was up there, standing beside him – and there was hardly room for three people to stand on that stone. It was the Cornet himself. Stooping, he grabbed the horn out of the Marshal's hand, and blew a blast on it. The chatter died away.

'Look,' he shouted. 'No use everybody talking at once. If this is all true, we've got to do something about it. Where are these sheep-stealers, laddie?'

Ken turned round, his back to the crowd, to face

93

southwards, looking into England. And then, his voice rising high, he pointed. 'There! There! That's where they are. That's Fiona guiding us.'

Clear enough to see, if one looked for it, though it seemed far, far away, a thin wisp of dark smoke blew eastwards from the top of one of the many lesser hills back there.

'Where? What? You mean yon smoke?' the Cornet asked.

'Yes. It's a signal. Like the Indians did. Or the balefires of the moss-troopers. I told her to light a fire about ten-thirty, to tell us where to come. The thieves will be below there, somewhere, with the sheep. Will you come and help to catch them?'

'By Jings, I will! We all will.' The Cornet blew on the horn again. 'Say, everybody! Who's coming wi' me? And wi' the laddie? To catch these crooks. It'll be the gang that's been lifting sheep for months. Who's game?'

A great cry went up – from the younger folk present, at any rate.

But there were other voices, too. Notably that of the Marshal.

'Hi, Dod!' he shouted. 'You canna dae that. It's the Common Riding. There's the offeecial pro-

94

gramme to stick to. We're due at Moss Tower by twelve noon.'

'To blazes wi' that!' the Cornet answered. He was only a plumber's apprentice, but clearly he knew his own mind. 'This is a chance we're no' going to miss.'

'Yes, Dod – but the Marshal's right too, you know,' the Provost put in. 'There's lots of people waiting for us, at various places, with hospitality and so on. This is a traditional ride. It's been done for hundreds of years. The Cornet and the Colours must make the round of the Marches. It's . . .'

'The Colours – okay. But no' the Cornet! No' just yet, anyway,' the young man cried. He turned, pointing to his Right-hand Man, who was holding the precious banner for him. 'Jockie – you've got the Flag. You take it. Carry it roond the Marches for me. You've done it before. You'll do it better'n me, anyway. You go wi' him, Provost. And the Marshal and the rest o' you. I'll join you later. Right now, I'm going wi' young Rutherford to put the fear o' death into these sheep-stealing crooks. And I guess a lot o' my supporters are coming wi' me!'

The roar of agreement that followed made it perfectly clear that he was not mistaken in that.

'Personally, I'm coming too, by Gad!' the General announced.

95

'Good for you, General!' The Cornet turned back to the Provost, earnestly. 'This is the *real* thing, Provost – d'you no' see? The Common Riding's grand – but it's sort o' shadow-boxing. Harking back to the old raids. This is a *genuine* Border raid. The Hot Trod, bang up to date!'

'Of course. I understand, Dod,' the Provost nodded. 'I . . . well, I just wish I was coming with you. But maybe I'm getting a bit old for that sort of thing. And in my position as Rulekirk's chief magistrate . . .'

'Oh, come *on*!' Ken interrupted. 'They may be getting away, while we talk here. And Fiona's all alone . . .'

'Sure, laddie,' the Cornet laughed. 'That's the spirit!' He blew a final blast on the horn, and then tossed it back to the rather glum-looking Marshal. 'Come on, all you that want a bit o' sport – follow me! Half come wi' me, and half go wi' the Colours and the Provost. To horse, boys – and ower the Border into Auld England! Yippeee!'

Far more than half the great throng of riders, a few moments later, were streaming southwards downhill after Ken and the Cornet, the General well to the fore.

CHAPTER NINE

To the Rescue

THEY made a wild and exciting ride of it, back over
the difficult country that Ken had covered so short
a time before. It was much rougher going than the
northern, grassy slopes up which the cavalcade had
ridden earlier, being full of bogs, peat-hags and old
heather, and cut up by burns and ravines. Soon the
sixty or seventy riders were widely strung out, for not
all of them were equally expert horsemen, and the
leaders were not hanging back for anybody. Ken was
lucky in having so spirited and game a horse as Demon.

Though soon the smoke from Fiona's fire died
away, they had picked on their landmarks and were
able to keep as straight a line as the ground would
allow. There were many slides and falls. One young
woman came off heavily when her mare slipped
down a bank and pitched her. Shaken and with a
strained shoulder she was escorted homewards by
two others who found the pace and the country a bit
too much for them. And a little later a youth got
bogged down in a peat mire, and his companions

themselves were somewhat the worse for wear before they got him and his beast out. They too turned back, having dropped far behind. At this rate, the party would thin out fairly rapidly.

After a very tough three-quarters of an hour the leading group were almost at the point where Ken had left Fiona, when, away ahead and slightly over to the left now, they saw a new column of smoke, from another small hill-top.

'I'd thought they would be making for the Tyne road again, farther down,' Ken panted. 'Looks as though they were swinging more to the east. Perhaps making for the Redesdale road instead – though it's an awful lot farther away.'

'Aye – but if they could get as far as Emblehope, there's a hill-road there all the way over to Redesdale,' the Cornet pointed out. 'It's no' a good road, mind – but they'd get lorries over it. Fifteen miles o' it.'

'That smoke is no more than three miles away,' the General cried. He had kept up very well, old man as he was, on a fine, tall sorrel hunter. 'Come along. Tally-ho!'

They raced on.

Twenty minutes later they pulled up on the long heathery ridge beside a dying fire, from which now

only a little blue curl of smoke rose. There was no sign of Fiona. And, gaze far and wide as they would, no sign of sheep or men either.

'Now, what?' the Cornet demanded. 'Which way?'

Before them, the ridge they were on sank away into a wide green space where three valleys met – the one from the west by which, no doubt, the sheep-stealers had come, and two others opening off north-east and south-east. These two were very different, steep-sided and narrow and twisting. The hills over that side, too, were of a totally different formation, rocky and harsh. The stolen flock could have taken either glen.

'Only thing to do is to go down, and look for

tracks,' Ken suggested. 'You can't drive over a hundred sheep without leaving tracks.'

'A pity,' the General said. 'We're better on the high ground. See farther. Those hills in front are too steep and craggy to ride over, too.'

'It can't be helped . . .'

They rode down into the wide, sunny hollow, slipping and slithering.

At the foot, the hills beyond looked even more grim and uninviting for horsemen, rising not very high but with sides of rock and scree and bare red earth that were almost cliffs. But at least they did not have to search hard for tracks and signs. Quite a large arrow, made of loose stones, pointed plainly into the more northerly of the two valleys.

'Good for the lassie!' the Cornet cried. 'She kens what she's doing, that one.'

'Yes.' Ken was proud of Fiona. But he was a bit worried, too. He pointed out, on a muddy stretch of the valley-floor, not only the tracks of sheep and men's boots, but also horse's hooves. Not very large ones. 'She's had to keep to the low ground now, too. She can't climb these jagged hills on a horse, either. So, if she's going to keep out of sight of the thieves, she'll have to hang back much farther.'

'Never mind,' the General said. 'So long as they

stick to the sheep, making all these tracks, we can't lose them.'

That was not altogether what was worrying Ken.

'No. But they may catch sight of her . . .' he said, doubtfully.

Strung out in a very long file they wound their way, as fast as they might, along that narrow, deep glen, beside a foaming burn under frowning, dark cliffs. It was never straight for more than a couple of hundred yards at a time, so they were never able to get any length of view. None of them knew the country well enough to guess for how long it might carry on this way.

And then, rounding a rocky bend, Ken pointed.

'There she is!' he exclaimed. 'There's Walter Scott!'

'Who . . .?'

'Walter Scott. That's my pony, that Fiona's riding.' The white pony was standing peacefully some distance ahead of them, beside a short and twisted thorn tree. 'She'll be hiding there.'

But when the riders came up to the pony, it was to find it tied to the bush – and no sign of Fiona. And there was nowhere round about that could hide her, save a number of big rock-falls at the foot of the hill. Surely she would never stay hidden behind there, now that Ken and his friends had arrived?

'She must have decided to go on, on foot,' the General suggested. 'Probably found that she could stalk them better . . .'

Ken had dismounted, and gone up the steep hillside a few yards to the big rocks. And suddenly he stopped, and turned.

'Look!' he called. 'There are men's tracks up here. Big boots. Fresh. And a cigarette-end. New. Quite dry. Men have been up here, waiting. That means hiding. What for? It must have been to catch Fiona! To ambush her!'

The others at the front of the column were off their horses now, searching around. Sure enough, they found other men's boot-marks a little way farther back, up behind more rocks. It was pretty clear what had happened. The thieves must have caught sight of the girl coming after them – probably they had been worried about her smoke-signals for a while. They had most likely driven the sheep on, round the bend, and then come back and hidden up above the valley-floor, in two groups of two men each. Then, when Fiona had come riding along, they had jumped up, and closed in on either side. In that narrow place, she would be unable to escape.

'They've got her!' Ken cried, very anxious now.

'They've taken her with them, for some reason. And tied up the pony. We've got to get after her. Rescue her. Quickly. They're bad men. Desperate. They might do anything . . .'

'They'll no' hurt the lassie, never fear,' the Cornet said – but not very confidently. 'Come on, then.'

Unhitching Walter Scott and taking him in tow, Ken pounded on. The leaders did not wait for him. Far behind, the long drawn-out string of riders came along.

About a mile farther on the valley was getting ever shallower but the sides were still as steep and craggy as ever. Ken, held back a little by the short-legged pony, was still a hundred yards or so behind the foremost riders. Rounding a tight bend in the glen, he heard a commotion in front. Amongst it was the baaing of sheep and the barking of dogs.

Round the corner, Ken was not prepared for the scene that met his eyes. The horsemen in front were hopelessly entangled and held up in a dense mass of sheep that completely filled the narrow bottom of the glen, milling about this way and that. Beyond them, and facing this way, three dogs barked and patrolled back and forward, allowing none of the flock to move farther up the valley. And high above the tight-packed, noisy block of protesting animals,

cursing, angry horsemen and yelping dogs, up on the top of the steep bank, four men stood on a small, thrusting shoulder of the hill. Two of them each held an arm of Fiona MacBride.

For a moment or two Ken was too upset to do more than stare and blink and bite his lip. Demon and Walter Scott were already surrounded by the struggling, steaming sheep, and had been forced to a halt. Above all the noise, Ken realized that one of the men up on the hill was shouting.

'. . . an' I ain't kiddin' you, neither,' he was calling down, in a rough but whining sort of voice, that certainly did not sound either Scots or good broad Northumbrian, decorated with sham American. 'You can't get up here with them hosses – an' we'll danged well roll down rocks on you if you try, see! We've got the girl, an' you've got the danged sheep! We'll leave the brutes, blast them – but we'll make it hot for the girl, by cripes! Unless you say you'll not follow us. Sure we'll take her – an' if you try comin' arter us, it won't be nice for her! Get it?'

'You dirty scum!' the General roared up at them, shaking his fist. 'You miserable low-down cowards! Using a young girl to hide behind . . .!'

'Sure, mister – an' we'll do more'n hide behind her, see. We ain't gonna be caught – that's flat. Try an' catch us, an' she suffers. Get that. Good an' hard she suffers. But give us your word there'll be no chasin' arter us, an' she can come right down to you. Safe an' sound, see. You got the choice, gents.'

The angry horsemen glared up at the man.

'Don't pay any attention to them – please!' called Fiona – and got a hard cuff across her head.

CHAPTER TEN

Fiona has the Last Word

AFTER the first, appalled few moments, Ken slid down from Demon's back, among the sheep. There were about a dozen riders in front of him, the nearest being only two or three yards away. To him he spoke.

'Hssst! I say—pass the word along. To keep talking. Go on. Tell them to keep them talking. Tell the Cornet and the General. Keep the thieves there. Please! Pass it on.'

The other rider, who was in fact the Cornet's Left-hand man, nodded, and turned in his saddle to speak to the man in front.

Ken, crouching as low as he could amongst the sheep, almost sickened by the heavy, hot, oily smell of the fleeces, turned also. He left his two horses standing there, and trying to keep them and the other riders between him and the thieves' line of vision, went dodging and jinking back the way he had just come. Another horseman had just come round the bend, staring wide-eyed at the scene, and to him Ken signed and pleaded to keep on, keep going forward towards the others, through the sheep. The man, who wore the colours of Hawick, looked mystified, but did as he was asked. Ken kept pressing on, hoping and praying that the men up on the hill did not see him.

With a sigh of thankfulness he rounded the bend in the glen, out of their sight. Straightening up, he went running down the path. Riders were coming along in ones and twos, as far as he could see down the glen. Sparing only a glance towards them, he stared up the steep hillside on his right, judging, searching.

He waved the first horseman to a stop.

'Quick!' he cried. 'Get down. There's trouble ahead. Can't explain fully now. We've got to get up this hill, somehow. Never do it on horses. They're just round the bend – captured Fiona. Holding us up. Only thing to do . . .'

Another rider came up – a young woman. Ken grabbed her bridle.

'Look. Stop all the others,' he panted. 'Don't let them round that bend. Tell them to climb up this hillside after us. The men, anyway. The thieves have got Fiona, and are threatening all sorts of things. You understand? Only thing for us to do is to get up this hill, and round behind them. On foot. A lot of us. See? They won't know there's a lot more of us round here, I don't think. You keep the horses. Tell them to hurry.'

The young woman began to ask a lot of questions, but Ken had no time to answer them. Fortunately she seemed to understand fairly well and was already turning her horse back towards the oncoming riders. Ken left her, and started at once to climb. The other man that he had stopped did not argue but came on after him on foot.

It was easier to talk about climbing that hillside than doing it. From the first it meant hands' and knees' work, on loose scree and rubble where the feet slid back two steps for every three taken. That was at the base. After that it got steeper and steeper, so that scree would not lie on it – only rock and bare red earth, with occasional tufts of rough grass growing here and there. It was just a question of choosing every step of the way, digging in toes here, pulling up by a tussock there, edging along sideways, working from one firm rock hold to another, meeting each problem as it came. Ken did not look down much. After the first dizzy glance below him, he decided that it was better to keep his eyes on the job. But he had noticed three or four others beginning to climb up after him already. His first companion was not following exactly in Ken's wake but finding his own way up.

It seemed farther up that cliff than it had appeared from below. The boy, gulping for breath, dragged and hauled and edged his way up. Living amongst hills, he had done much climbing – but this was more like mountaineering. There must be an easier way, farther along, he decided – where the thieves and Fiona had climbed up. No doubt they had waited till they found just such a place before they set their trap.

Ken reached a belt of bare rock, quite a dozen feet high, with little or no soil to cover it. It was almost sheer too – in fact, to his left, it actually overhung slightly. He tried hard to find a way up, to seek out crevices and cracks in the rock for hand holds, and projections for toe holds. But though there were one or two to take him a little way, there were not enough to get him up and over. Helplessly he hung there, fretting with impatience. He realized that it was no use. He would have to go back. And getting down where he had just come up was no joke in itself, and such a waste of time. Clinging desperately, he began to work his way down again.

A shout from his right, and higher, showed him

his first companion who had found a better way up over this rock-face, and was now above it, leaning down and pointing, to guide Ken. Thankfully the boy worked his way along to this route. He found it much easier – especially when the man held out a hand to him and helped pull him up the last bit. Puffing and panting, he crouched there on the edge for a moment. Higher, the hillside sloped back at an easy angle.

But Ken could not wait, breathless as he was.

'You stay here. Guide the others up,' he gasped to his unknown friend. 'I'll go on. That way.' And he pointed. 'Keep an eye on them. When you've got enough people, bring them along. After me. Keep well back, out of sight. Round that heather hum-mock. You see? As quick as you can. I'll wave to you – guide you.'

He glanced down. There were quite a knot of horses and a few riders down at the foot now, some girls amongst them, and fully eight or ten men at various stages of the climb up. 'Bring that lot. Eight at least. There are four thieves – but they're des-perate.'

'Och, aye,' the other answered grimly. 'Man, I'll take on any two o' them, my ain sel'!'

Leaving him, Ken ran back eastwards, keeping

that heathery mound that he had pointed out between him and where he reckoned the sheep-stealers
had been placed. He was hoping that the others had
managed to keep them there, talking.

He found a fold in the hillside up there, once he
was round the hummock, which led him along out
of sight well enough. When he believed that he had
gone far enough, he crept up to the edge of it on
hands and knees. He found that he had not gone
as far as he had
thought. The four
men and Fiona, their
backs to him, were still
nearly a hundred
yards away. But at
least they were still
there. One of them
seemed to be shouting.

Anxiously Ken
peered back. No sign
of his friends yet. He
hurried farther along,
behind the little ridge,
and then crawled up
again. He was right
behind the enemy

now, and perhaps fifty yards back from their position. He lay there, in the heather, switching his gaze from their backs to where he looked for his supporters. He hoped that the thieves would not turn round yet – not until his friends turned up.

Two of the crooks seemed to be having an argument. One of them quite obviously was for bolting right away – presumably with Fiona. One of the others seemed to be siding with him. It was quite clear that they were all getting tired of the talk from below.

Ken chewed a heather-stem in a fever of impatience. Would his people never come? What on earth could they be doing all this time?

As it happened, both moves came at exactly the same moment. The thieves, after a last fist-shaking shout at the people below them, turned, pulling Fiona round roughly between them, and began to come hurrying up the hill. And just then, as his heart sank, Ken saw out of the corner of his eye, a tight group of breeched and booted riders coming running along the same fold in the hill that he had used.

Almost gibbering with excitement he slid his way back from the crest of his little ridge, and got to his feet, once out of sight from the front, waving wildly, furiously, for the others to hurry. He reckoned that

they were almost twice as far away as the thieves –
a hundred yards to fifty. He jerked his clenched fist
up and down, in the motion that means hurry.

Seeing him, the horseless horsemen redoubled
their efforts, running just as hard and fast as riding-
boots and spurs will allow amongst high, old heather,
tripping and stumbling. There seemed to be a great
lot of them; though Ken did not count them, there
were actually thirteen.

The moments seemed to pass in an agony of slow-
ness. Why the thieves had not appeared over the
ridge Ken could not imagine – until he remembered
that they were coming uphill, which was always
slower, and in long heather also. And they had
Fiona to hustle along, who certainly would not be
hurrying, if she could help it.

In his agitation, Ken ran a few yards to meet his
friends.

'Quick!' he cried. 'Oh, quick! They're just coming. Four of them. Any moment they'll appear.
Over there. Quick – link arms. So's to face them
with a barrier . . .'

But they did not have time to do any such thing.
As they swung round, in a red-faced, panting bunch,
to face the little heather ridge, the four sheep-
stealers, Fiona still between them, appeared from

113

over the other side of it, directly in front, and not ten
yards away. Both sides stopped dead. It was a dra-
matic meeting.

But that was all the drama that was in it, in fact.
At the sight of all these new enemies, three times
their own number, and obviously entirely un-
expected, the crooks just folded up. One of them,
certainly, did try to bolt on his own, but two sturdy
Borderers, evidently rugby men, hurled themselves
headlong at him, tackling him round the knees, and
brought him down with a crash. His companions
stood where they were, motionless. All except
Fiona, who, jerking herself free, came running
forward.

'Ken! Ken!' she cried. 'Good for you! I knew
you'd manage it somehow.'

'You're all right, Fiona? They've . . . they've not
hurt you?'

'No. No – I'm fine. Really . . .'

'Sure, she's all right. We never hurt the kid,' the
thieves' spokesman said hurriedly, his voïce more
whining than ever. 'Did we, missy? We jest took her
along with us for a bit. Case she got lost, see . . .'

'Quiet, you!' one of the older riders said sternly.
'I'm a magistrate – a J.P. Any more talking you can
do to the police. Are you coming quietly – or do

you want the treatment, like your pal in the heather?'

'Okay, okay – we ain't makin' no trouble, guv'nor. Honest. We'll go quietly.'

'Well, remember that.'

Fiona, both hands gripping Ken's arm, was actually jumping up and down in her excitement and delight, eyes shining. 'Oh, Ken! Oh, Ken!' was all she could find to say.

The boy liked her very much, and was very happy too. But he coughed, just the same. 'I say . . .' he said. 'My arm, Fiona! H'rrr'mm. It's jolly good, and all that, I know. But . . .' He glanced round at all the grinning red faces. 'D'you mind letting go of my arm . . .?'

Nearly four hours later, weary, travel-stained and saddle-sore, the main portion of the Cornet's cavalcade paced into the cobbled, narrow streets of the old grey town of Rulekirk. They paced, rather than trotted, not so much because the horses were tired, as for reasons of showmanship. The Cornet thought that it would be a good idea to set down the prisoners, who up till then had been forced to ride pillion behind tough members of the company, and make them trudge through the crowded streets on foot, tied together and hands bound behind their backs. It would be something new in the traditions of the Common Riding, though the police might not allow that for very long.

They had seven prisoners now, for they had come back by the hidden lorries at the Deadwater, and had been lucky enough to ambush the three drivers there, returning from their long quest for new rotors. Thereafter they had halted at the first roadside telephone kiosk they had come to, and phoned the good news to Rulekirk, saying approximately when they hoped to arrive in the town. Ken had also rung up his parents at Houndlaw, to their great relief – though it appeared that the Provost had already telephoned them from Moss Tower, about Ken's exciting arrival at the Rescue Stone on Peel Fell.

And so, to the ringing cheers of the crowds, the fifty or so horsemen, with Ken and Fiona riding first behind the Cornet in the place of honour, paced through the little town. The Right-hand man had met them at the outskirts with the Colours, which he handed back to the Cornet, who now carried the historic banner fluttering proudly in the lead. At the High Street the town band was waiting for them, and started up the stirring strains of the Common Riding song, to march at their head to the town hall.

There, on a gaily decorated platform, the Provost and all the bigwigs and official guests stood waiting to receive them, and to receive the burgh's flag back into safe keeping for another year. So ended all Common Ridings – but surely never before one quite the same as this. Those sheep-stealers may have been hardened criminals, but it is unlikely that they had ever had such a public demonstration that crime does not pay. If there was any sheepishness about that afternoon, it was they who showed it, as they shuffled miserably along between the horsemen, eyes downcast on the cobblestones.

The cheering and singing rose to a great shout as the procession reached the square and the town hall. Ken saw his father and mother in the group on the platform behind the Provost, and waved excitedly, pointing them out to Fiona on Walter Scott. Press photographers were busy with their cameras.

The Provost made a speech, of course. He had to, to welcome the Cornet and the Colours home, but very quickly he got over the official bit. Then he looked at Ken and Fiona, smiling.

'The Cornet is the hero of the Common Riding – and must always be,' he said. 'And this year's Cornet has lived up to the highest traditions of his ancient office. But, I must say, he has serious rivals this time for the place of hero. We have two young people here, who . . .'

He could not make himself heard for the din of cheering and shouting. Ken looked extremely un-comfortable, and Fiona blushed scarlet.

118

The Provost tried again. 'Young Ken Rutherford and his friend Fiona have done . . .'

Again the storm of hurrays and applause drowned his words. People pressed forward, to surge round the young folk, horses or none. Demon, always excitable, began to get restless – though Walter Scott stood as wisely quiet as in his own stall at Houndlaw.

'. . . very, very proud of these youngsters . . .' the Provost's voice could just be heard.

'I say,' Ken said, to Fiona, trying to soothe Demon at the same time. 'This is awful! D'you think we could get out of here?'

'But, why? I think it's rather nice,' the girl said. 'I thought you liked the Common Riding, Ken?'

'That's different. This is just, just crazy!'

'. . . we all hope, I'm sure . . . one day . . . young Ken Rutherford . . . a future Cornet . . .'

More and more cheers.

Ken looked about him desperately. The Marshal had appeared close by on his big roan, possibly to try to keep order in the pressing crowd about the youngsters. On an impulse, Ken reached out and grabbed his horn from its case at the man's saddle. He put it to his lips, and blew.

It was not a terribly successful blast, but it did make a high, piercing sort of shriek that penetrated above the hullabaloo and produced a sudden silence. Into the hush, Ken's voice spoke, a little shrilly.

'Look,' he said. 'If you don't watch out, those thieves will escape in the crush! I must say, I think the police ought to grab them, instead of having to control all you people! Now – will you watch out! Out of the road! Because Fiona and I are going home. We're absolutely ravenous!' And grabbing Walter Scott's bridle, he pulled both horses round.

Hastily, amid great laughter, people scattered out of the way, right and left. And into the space the two young folk swung, to go clattering down the High Street and away, Demon high-stepping and eager still, Walter Scott almost in dignified protest. Cheer after cheer rang out behind them, following them out of town.

'Gosh!' Ken cried. 'I've never been so embarrassed in my life. No more thief-catching for me!'

'I . . . see what you mean . . . about Brave Borderland . . . now, Ken,' Fiona got out, as they jerked along. 'Peaceful wasn't . . . quite the right word . . . was it?'